HOT IN WITCH CITY

SALEM SUPERNATURALS 2

LISA CARLISLE

LISACARLISLEBOOKS

HOT IN WITCH CITY

A wolf shifter thinks I'm his mate.

Not going to happen.

I'm half-siren and all single. No way am I giving up my freedom for some delusional furball.

Even if he's kind of cute. And considerate. And has warm eyes.

Besides, I have enough going on with running my retro rock club. And when an unexpected relative shows up there one night, it shakes me to the core.

The last thing I need is to add another complication to my life, especially something as mundane as monogamy.

Fans of New Girl and What We Do in the Shadows will love the Salem Supernaturals series - paranormal chick lit romances with a splash of romance, comedy, and mystery!

For E. Always.

THE EPILOGUE FROM REBEL SPELL

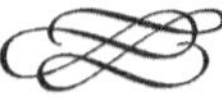

As a refresher, here's the epilogue from book 1, *Rebel Spell. Hot in Witch City* continues that same night.

Enjoy!

~Lisa

SEBASTIAN

Nova convinced us to visit her friend Gianna's club, Danger Zone, to celebrate our next chapter as housemates. Nova and Diego had gone to New York for the weekend. When they returned, they officially moved her into the house.

Lucas and I followed them into the club. Who would have thought these two would get together? Certainly not me when they'd first met. Not after Diego had been almost out of control with a thirst for her blood.

I smirked at how he'd wrapped his arm protectively around her waist. He must have been hungry for something else as well.

We entered the club, a dark room with red and purple lights shining overhead. Billy Idol's "Rebel Yell" played, and many of the women pumped their arms as they chanted along with, "More, more, more."

I nudged Lucas. "A good sign for us getting lucky tonight."

He nodded and arched his brows. "Indeed." Pointing to the bar, he said, "Let's get a drink first."

Once we sat at the bar and ordered drinks, I caught it—the scent that had been driving me crazy in recent weeks. "I smell it. Right here in this club."

It wasn't a bad smell, quite the opposite. It was alluring.

I'd scented it on Nova—sometimes.

I'd scented it in our kitchen.

And now, I scented it here, more pronounced than ever.

"Enough with that already." Diego rolled his eyes. "You keep talking about this 'scent.' It must all be in your head."

"No." I shook my head. "It started after Nova came into town." I glanced at her.

She tilted her head and teased. "Sorry, Sebastian. Not sure what it means, but I'm taken."

"That's not it. It's not you," I replied. Then what exactly was it?

It was stronger here than in the past. So feminine and enchanting. Whoever this woman was, she'd been in this spot recently. I scanned the women dancing, moving their bodies with wild abandon as they jumped around to the song.

Unable to sit still, I downed my shot of whiskey and climbed off the stool. Would I finally unravel the identity of this mysterious woman?

"Where are you going?" Lucas asked.

"To find her," I declared. "Whoever she is, wherever she is, I'm tracking her down tonight."

CHAPTER 1

GIANNA

Showtime.

The red and purple lights shined overhead, the retro rock music encouraged the crowd out to dance, and the bartenders were busy. My club was already packed, a good sign for the night. I wandered through the crowd, greeting regulars. A flash of auburn hair on a petite woman caught my attention. I headed over to my closest friend and the three guys walking with her.

"Nova!" I greeted her and bent down to hug her.

She grinned. "Hey, Gianna."

I was so happy to have her back in Salem. She'd been living in New York and had only moved back recently after inheriting her estranged aunt's house. Salem hadn't been the same without her.

I didn't blame her for leaving, as I'd also left town as soon as we graduated. After a few years, I missed this strange little town that tolerated supernaturals as long as we laid low and didn't cause any havoc.

After we pulled apart, I said. "Perfect timing. Listen."

The opening beats of one of our favorite songs, "When Doves Cry," pounded from the speakers. We were both huge Prince fans and had played the *Purple Rain* album countless times. Music was one thing we bonded over. Being outcasts was another.

We sang the chorus together and then laughed. I glanced at the guys accompanying her, her tenants, and recognized her vampire boyfriend with his dark hair and serious blue eyes.

"Diego," I greeted him.

He and I had formed a quick friendship after a life-threatening situation last month when he'd helped Nova rescue me from a demon, an encounter I didn't want to remember. Ever. Being controlled in any way was my greatest fear. Being held captive by a demon on a power trip amped that terror to a phobia.

"Looks like business is good, Gianna," Diego acknowledged with a nod.

"Indeed." I smiled with pride. I was proud of *Danger Zone*, the club I'd opened north of Boston. It had taken a ton of hard work and hard-earned cash, but it flourished enough for me to make a down payment on a townhouse in Salem. With my business and my place, I'd finally achieved the independence I'd craved. Nothing and no one was going to change that.

"This is Lucas." Nova gestured to the guy with chin-length blond hair and a toothpaste model smile.

Three supernatural guys rented out the main part of the house, while Nova lived in a separate section where her aunt had lived.

"Ah, the dragon shifter," I said in a lower tone. I'd heard plenty about her tenants, including this fun-loving guy who worked as an exotic dancer.

"Technically, only half shifter." Lucas winked. "But full of fire." He took my hand and kissed it. "Enchante."

I laughed. "Have we transported to eighteenth-century France?"

He arched a brow. "We can go wherever you'd like to travel, milady."

Ah, he was living up to his reputation as a flirt.

Nova motioned behind her. "And this is Sebastian."

This guy was as dark as Lucas was light and had a full beard. His expression was dead serious, the opposite of Lucas's friendly smile.

"Hey, Sebastian." I greeted him with a pleasant smile.

His mouth opened, but nothing came out. He stared at me, and I sighed. This wasn't unusual. I attributed this effect to my siren blood. What exactly that meant, I didn't know for sure. My mother had abandoned me soon after I was born and took with her all the answers to the questions about that side of me. I'd never forgive her for it.

His nostrils flared, and he gazed at me with curiosity, like I was an undiscovered flower species.

Sebastian stepped closer—too close. Into my personal space.

When he sniffed me, I backed away. "What are you doing?"

"It's you," he declared with a fascinated but wary glance. "You're the one who's been driving my wolf crazy."

I huffed. "I don't know what you're talking about, Sebastian, since we haven't met until now." Planting my hands on my hips, I said, "Quite an odd first impression, I might add."

"Sebastian, what's going on?" Nova's voice edged up a notch.

His eyes flashed with amber amid the dark brown, and he leaned closer. "It's your scent." He inhaled once more. "I know it. I've smelled it at our house and—" he glanced around, "—here at the club."

"Dude, you're acting strange." Diego nudged Sebastian's arm.

A low, vibrating growl rumbled from his chest.

"Get yourself under control," Lucas warned under his breath.

Holy tridents. I pointed at Sebastian's chest. "Are you insane? You can't let your animal side out in public."

Sebastian's eyes glowed brighter, almost golden, as he stared at me. He released a low, mournful moan that sounded more wolf than human. "Mine."

"Oh no," I groaned and stepped back. A possessive wolf. "I'm most definitely *not* yours. And don't even think about shifting in here."

It would be bad for business. Even though supernaturals were welcome in my club, they knew better than to reveal their true nature to all.

"I won't," he snarled.

"You better not," I warned. Glancing at the perimeter of the club, I noted the locations of the bouncers, just in case this situation escalated.

"*Mae—*" Whatever Sebastian was saying rolled from him with a vibrating tone, before he cut it off and his eyes widened with surprised horror.

"Sebastian, are you okay?" Nova asked.

His mouth twisted as he appeared to wrestle for some self-control. "My wolf is all amped up. I'll get him to calm down."

"Please do—and fast," I snapped, my patience wearing thin with this weirdo. "This is my club, and I don't need any shifter drama."

Sebastian blinked at me and then gritted his teeth. The unnatural golden hue faded from his eyes. "I'm sorry, Gianna. That was rude of me." He raised his chin. "Let me start over." He smiled. "I'm a chef."

That shift in his disposition was faster than holding a mood ring over a mug of steaming tea. He looked much friendlier than he had a second ago. His rugged handsomeness might have caught my attention if he hadn't acted so strange. I lifted a brow. "That's nice."

"You like to eat?"

I laughed without mirth. "What an odd question. Who doesn't?"

He pointed to his chest. "I make good food." His tone was well-suited for the prehistoric era.

"What are you, a caveman?" I teased, calling him out.

He shook his head. "Err, I mean, I can cook you a nice meal, Gianna."

"That's okay, Chef Boyardee." I wagged a finger. "Just try to avoid making a scene tonight."

I turned to walk away, but he grabbed my hand. "Don't leave yet."

I pulled my hand back. "Don't grab me." I walked away from them and straight behind the bar, muttering, "possessive wolf."

Something about the shifter rattled me, starting the moment he'd declared me *his*. I'd spent years clashing with my father, a former Marine and current control freak, in my quest for independence. I was not anyone's, least of all a stranger who sauntered into my club and almost shifted in public.

Frustration simmering, I poured myself a Peaches, the champagne cocktail that was my current beverage of choice. After I took a hearty sip and swallowed the cool bubbly liquid, I exhaled. That was better.

I helped take care of a few drink orders since the bartenders had patrons lined up three deep and then walked away with my glass.

How could Nova tolerate this guy? She'd said such good things about her tenants. Color me unimpressed.

Nova caught up with me as I walked through the club. "I don't know what's gotten into Sebastian. Diego and Lucas are going to talk some sense into him."

I shook my head. "Ugh, what a weirdo, sniffing and pawing at me."

Nova bit her lip. "He's not like this. He's usually super considerate, wanting to cook up a storm to feed us."

I snorted, remembering his odd offer to cook for me.

Nova tipped her head with a knowing grin. "It's not like you haven't had an odd effect on men before."

True. Men had been attracted to me ever since I'd transformed from an awkward caterpillar to a butterfly after puberty.

"But he looked ready to shift in my club. That would be bad for business."

"Absolutely," Nova agreed. "Diego and Lucas will keep him in check."

When I glanced back they were talking to Sebastian. He stared at me with an odd expression that I could only guess was confusion—and maybe yearning.

I turned away and muttered, "Furball freak."

SEBASTIAN

"W**HAT ARE YOU DOING, DUDE**?" Diego stepped in my path as I tried to follow Gianna.

Nova had told me about her good friend who lived in Salem, but she'd left out the fact that Gianna was a knockout. She stood tall on sexy high heels that showed off her long legs. Her pinup-style black dress with red bats printed on them matched the crimson streaks in her dark hair. Her captivating eyes were a mysterious color somewhere between dark blue and purple. And her body… Wowza.

"You sounded *real smooth*," Lucas added with a chuckle.

I scowled. "It's her," I explained. "Her scent is the one that's been driving me mad." That feminine aroma with a hint of vanilla had haunted me for weeks. It lured me to pursue, yet eventually vanished, leaving me confused and bereft.

And acting so, as well, judging by the idiotic display I'd just put on. Muttering "mine" and spouting off gibberish about food and cooking. My wolf had to settle down. I'd barely been able to cut off the word "mate" from escaping my mouth as it rumbled from deep within.

"Uh, oh." Lucas bent his head down. "You're not saying what I *think* you're saying, are you?" He lowered his voice. "Mate?"

"No. No, of course not," I dismissed. "I don't know." I averted eye contact and ran my hand over my beard. My wolf told me she was indeed the one, but I didn't know if I believed it.

Or maybe I didn't want to believe it.

As a wolf shifter who'd grown up with a pack in the White Mountains, I'd heard the stories about what happens when a shifter finds a mate. Everything changed. She'd be the missing half to your soul. All this woo-woo magic transpired, making you feel whole.

I thought when I found my mate, I'd know it without a doubt. Everything would fall into place.

That didn't happen. Instead, confusion reigned. Restlessness had built up since I'd first detected the unfamiliar scent in our house. Could I really fall that fast and hard for a stranger I'd never met before simply by smelling her? That was ludicrous, and I had to be sensible about something as huge as a life partner.

"She's part siren," Diego said. "Maybe that's affecting you somehow."

Could that be it? She had siren magic stirring my wolf, confusing him?

"That explains it," I declared with more confidence than I felt. "False alarm," I dismissed. She was *not* my mate. My wolf snorted in disagreement.

That magical sense of fulfillment from finding a mate had to be another falsehood my former pack had fed me. They lived a backwards life, and I should have known better than to believe anything they said.

"Now that we got that out of the way." Lucas pointed with both index fingers at the bar. "Drinks."

"Indeed." We were in a club and our hands were empty.

Diego led us to the opposite side of the bar from where Nova stood talking to Gianna. Damn, she was beautiful. I couldn't stop staring at her.

"Knock it off," Diego warned. "You're going to freak her out."

"Right, right." I blinked. Already this woman was wreaking havoc on me, causing my wolf to react with unfamiliar yearning.

She *couldn't* be my mate. She just couldn't. I wouldn't change my entire lifestyle over a woman I'd just met, even if she was super hot. Big deal. I'd met many beautiful women, and they didn't scowl at me and then turn away the way Gianna had.

That's what I should do to refocus—find someone else. Someone who didn't provoke such a strong reaction that made me act out of character, sniffing and snarling in public like a wolf lost to the full moon.

My wolf growled, not on board with that plan, but I was the one in charge. I wouldn't succumb to my animal side. I'd left the pack for a more civilized life, and that's how I intended to continue.

That meant no more talk of mates. I was much better off with a warmer reception from a friendly face rather than someone who recoiled when I touched her.

Lucas ordered a Gin Blossom, their take on a gin and tonic, and I chose a Gorky Park, their version of a Moscow mule. Diego leaned forward and asked for his in a hushed tone. The bartender nodded and returned with a crimson drink, probably including blood.

I nudged Lucas. "Let's get back in the game."

"That's more like it," he responded with a wide, approving grin. He rubbed his hands together. "Bring on the hotties."

Diego snorted and then raised his glass. "Have fun."

Lucas and I wandered around the club to check out the ladies there tonight. Diego walked over to Nova and Gianna. My wolf moaned, nudging me to go back to her, but I gritted my teeth and ignored him. I wouldn't be led around by my wolf, who ran more on instinct than sense.

When the song changed up to Lenny Kravitz's "Are You Gonna Go My Way," we slipped onto the dance floor where a group of four pretty women were dancing. We danced nearby, moving closer, and they moved out to let us into their circle. Nice.

I glanced at Gianna, who was talking to Nova and Diego, across the club. My gaze cruised over her fine curves wrapped in a slinky black dress. My wolf growled in impatience. I ached to return to her.

Wrestling my gaze away, I focused on the fine females who looked ready to have fun.

Mate, my wolf insisted.

No, you're wrong.

When I glanced up halfway through the song, she was gone. A sinking sensation followed.

I pushed through with halfhearted movements until the end of the song. Dancing was futile. I nodded to Lucas. "I'm going back to the bar." Waving at the group, I added, "Have a great night, ladies."

I headed back toward the bar. Diego and Nova weren't there.

Samantha Fox's "Naughty Girls Need Love, Too," played next. Gianna headed out to the dance floor, raising her arms as if declaring this was her song.

A tall guy with tattooed sleeves stepped up to her. She didn't seem to mind and danced with him. Jealousy ripped through my gut like claws.

I retreated away from them but couldn't stop watching. Why was she smiling and dancing with *him?* It should have been me. The more I stared, the sharper the torment grew within.

Why? I didn't even know this damn woman!

Frustrated, I gritted my teeth and rubbed my beard. Coming here was a mistake. Finding the source of the mystery woman had only made things more confusing.

When he slid his hand around her waist, it twisted me in agony. My heart pounded, and the bass thumped in my ears.

A few beats later, she spun out of his grasp and turned away, slipping in to dance with others. I exhaled.

He didn't give her much space and crept up on her. My fingers clenched halfway to fists. When he pulled her close, sliding his leg in between hers as if trying out as an extra for *Dirty Dancing,* her expression darkened. She stepped away and raised her index finger, appearing to tell him to back off.

For maybe the duration of the chorus, he made his boorish dance moves on other women. They quickly scooted away from him. By the end of the song, he'd slunk back to Gianna, mimicking humping motions from behind. My teeth clenched against each other like the dragging of tectonic plates.

He grabbed her hips and dry humped her. She struggled to slip out of his hold.

My vision was vividly bathed in crimson, and fury ripped through my body.

I pushed past anyone who stood in the way. I pulled the guy away from her. Turning toward me, he shouted, "What the hell?"

"Don't touch her." I pulled my fist back and punched him in the face.

As he recoiled, I pushed him to the ground.

Shouts rang over the music, including Gianna's "What are you doing?"

Good freakin' question. I'd never been in a bar brawl, let alone initiated a fight. My scraps had typically been attempting to defend myself from the older boys who'd picked on me when I was in the pack.

The guy I'd punched recovered from the shock and fought back. We scuffled, rolling over each other on the sticky floor, trying to land another punch.

Someone dragged me backwards.

"He's out." Gianna pointed behind me.

Diego and Nova rushed over as I was hauled away. I struggled to rush forward and continue the fight with the guy. Other bouncers pulled him in the other direction.

"What's going on?" Diego asked.

Gianna's face turned into a mask of fury. "Get your feral friend out of here!"

CHAPTER 2

SEBASTIAN

The next morning, I had the biggest hangover of my life—not one from drinking too much alcohol, but from a night of swallowing regret. I peered at the spinning blades in my ceiling fan. Although it was December in New England, I ran hot. It was part of my wolf nature.

My wolf. Damn troublemaker. What had gotten into him last night?

An image of Gianna appeared before me, and I pictured her beautiful smile and lush curves. Too bad soon after I'd opened my mouth, the smile left her face. Her expression had been pulled into one of confusion, wariness, or downright fury, and all because of me.

Smooth.

I climbed out of bed and put on a pair of black sweats and then went into the bathroom. When I washed up, I stared at myself in the mirror. My hair and beard were bedraggled, and my eyes appeared tormented. That was spot on for the mood of the morning. While I groomed myself, I relived the mortification and inner turmoil.

Although I'd always thought finding my mate would bring about some inner peace and sense of completeness, what happened last night was anything but that. My wolf was wilder than ever and urging, *go find her.*

Enough of his nonsense. Especially if he was going to make us act like a primitive beast unfit to live in society.

After last night's epic disaster, one thing was clear—I didn't want a mate.

My wolf roared his feelings on that matter. Tough. I was the one in charge.

Bounding down the stairs, I headed into the kitchen. There was no sign of anyone else up yet. That was good—I was sure to be peppered with more questions about what had gotten into me last night.

While I prepared steak, eggs, and coffee, I thought about what to do that day since I wasn't working until later that afternoon. What I should do was let my wolf out to run and burn off some of the restlessness. Maybe that was the cause of the recent chaos —I hadn't let him roam free and hunt enough, so it was taking a toll on both of us. We'd go out after dark.

In the meantime, I'd do what I could to burn through the excess energy. After I ate, I headed to the gym. Physical exertion might help tear the mortification and regret of that encounter with Gianna out of my head.

Two hours of sweating with cardio and weights and finishing up with the sauna and a long shower passed. Distraction hadn't worked. My mind was assaulted with repeated visions of her. How could I deal with this unwanted intrusion?

The only thing that came to mind was that I had to first, take care of my wolf's agitation, and second, see Gianna again. That way, he'd see it was all a mix-up. She was just a hot woman who smelled good. Nothing more.

When I returned home, I had to face up to my actions last night. I knocked on the door of Nova's apartment.

"Come in," she called.

Once I entered, I glanced at the space. Each time I stopped by, Nova had put more of a stamp on her aunt's apartment in her own style. The walls had a fresh coat of paint, a shade of sky blue. A hint of the fresh paint odor lingered.

Nova and Diego sat on the sofa, each holding a mug and staring at me with a questioning look. Nova wore red plaid lounge pants and a pale-blue hoodie, and her hair was pulled into a side braid. Diego wore black sweats and a long-sleeve gray shirt. Mr. Colorful, as always.

"We were just talking about you," Nova said. "You okay, Sebastian?"

I lowered my head. "Sorry I was an ass last night."

"What got into you, man?" Diego drank from his mug and the familiar blood-tinged coffee fragrance wafted over.

I scowled as I sat in an armchair. "It was my wolf. You know I'm not like that."

"What was it about Gianna's scent?" Nova asked. "You kept talking about it."

"My wolf was confused," I explained.

Inside, he snorted in disagreement.

"Maybe it was her siren blood," Nova said. "Guys are drawn to her and can act—" She turned her hand palm up. "Well, like dumbasses." She smiled.

That pretty much nailed it. "Maybe," I answered in a noncommittal tone. "Don't worry, Nova. I'm a lover, not a fighter." I gestured to myself and grinned.

"Could have fooled me," she replied in a sing-song voice.

True. My actions didn't back up my words. "Is she pissed at me?"

"She was last night," Nova replied. "I texted her this morning, but she hasn't replied yet."

"Of course she is," Diego added. "You started a brawl at her club."

A low vibration rumbled from my chest.

Diego scoffed. "Don't growl at me." He put his mug down on a coaster.

"I'm not growling at you. Just letting off some steam." I turned back to Nova. "When are you going to see her again?"

"No plans at the moment." Nova shrugged. "But probably soon."

"How soon?"

"Easy, Sebastian," she replied. "What's with the rush?"

"I want to apologize about my behavior last night."

Nova sipped from her mug. "I can pass on the message."

"It's better in person."

Nova assessed me while she held the mug in both hands, as if savoring the warmth. "I don't know if that's a good idea."

"Why not?"

"Do we have to remind you how you were escorted out on your ass last night?" Diego said.

I raised my hand. "Hence, the apology I'm trying to make."

"We'll see," Nova said. "I'm busy with the Network and preparing for the Winter Solstice."

She was being trained to work at the Salem Supernatural Network while also working virtually for a children's editor in New York. I'd met Diego and Lucas through the Network as they helped supernaturals find housing and jobs in a human world.

"Gianna will be busy preparing for a New Year's Eve bash at the club," Nova added.

Oh, that could be a perfect opportunity to see Gianna again, although next week seemed so far away. "Are you going?"

"Yes," Nova replied. "We both are." She motioned to Diego and then herself.

"I want to come."

Diego snort laughed. "I'm sure Gianna would be thrilled to welcome you back after last night."

"The new year is a new start," I countered with a wave. "You can't hold grudges into a new year."

"Says who?" Diego asked.

"It sounded like it came out of my mouth," I replied.

"How are you going to explain this to Gianna, anyway?" Diego furrowed his brows. "That her scent drove your wolf batty?"

I shot him a look. "Do you really want to go there? Shall we go over how feral you went when you first smelled Nova? How you wanted to taste her blood right in our living room?"

"Is that what happened?" Nova turned to him with an inquisitive look. "I thought it was because you were pissed that I might be selling the house."

Diego scowled at me. "Thanks, man." He turned to Nova. "You know how crazy your scent makes me. That first time, well—it took me by surprise."

"Oh, Diego." Nova tilted her head as she gave him a small smile.

While they exchanged a googly eyed glance, I turned away. The last thing I wanted to see was them making out in front of me, turned on by Diego's blood fetish.

"Can you invite Gianna over?" I interrupted before they went at it on the sofa.

Nova pulled her gaze to me. "Why?"

"I told you, I want to apologize in person. Might as well do it sooner than later." Searching for something to offer, I added, "Better yet—I'll cook us dinner."

"What if you wolf out again?" Diego asked.

"I won't. I'll take my wolf out for a run. That's probably what all this restlessness is about."

"I'll think about it," Nova replied.

That could lead to a no, so I had to persist.

"What's there to think about? It's food. This way we can meet up properly and break bread. We all need to eat." With a wry grin at my vampire roommate who had a stomach the size of a worm, I added, "Even if some of us prefer a liquid diet."

"Stop being pushy," Diego said.

"Stop being overprotective."

"You're badgering Nova," Diego replied.

"Nova took on a demon. I don't think me asking a question about dinner is going to send her over the edge."

"Stop arguing about stupid things," Nova said with an exaggerated eye roll. "Why are you being so adamant about this?"

"I feel horrible about last night," I explained. "That's not how I am. And besides, she's your best friend, and I'm your house mate. We're obviously going to run into each other. We might as well get this little uncomfortable snafu out of the way so we can all hang out without any awkwardness."

"All right, we'll see," Nova replied.

"When?" I asked.

"Enough with the pressure," Diego warned.

I raised my hand. "I'm just being practical. Dinner preparation takes planning."

"Jeez," Nova said. "I'm sure I'll hear back from her today. I'll bring it up and let you know."

I smiled at the small victory. I'd come over here ashamed but had worked out one small step that got me closer to seeing Gianna again. My wolf would realize that what he'd sensed in the club was a fluke.

Then I could move on with my life without him pestering me to claim a stranger as my mate.

GIANNA

After lunch, I headed over to the beach to clear my head. I tried to walk near water at least once a week, preferably the ocean. Although it was cool in December, I could withstand chilly temperatures more than most humans.

A cool breeze rolled from the sea, but the sky was clear and cloudless, making it a sunny afternoon. The light gleamed on the calm ripples of the ocean. I was the only one along this stretch of sand. Sometimes there were people walking their dogs, but in the winter, I had more time alone to walk and think. The club could get loud and busy, and I enjoyed the tranquility with the sound of the ocean and its familiar comforting scent.

In addition to spending time near the water, I loved to swim as much as possible. I swam laps at my gym's pool two or three times a week and had gone earlier that morning. My father had signed me up for lessons when I was young, one of the rare times he nurtured my siren side. It came natural to me, and I joined the swim team in grade school, continuing until I graduated. The motion of gliding through the water invigorated and calmed me.

My phone buzzed, and when I glanced at the caller, it was Nova. "Hey, lady," I greeted her.

"Hi, Gianna. What are you up to?"

"Walking the beach. Clearing out all the mental clutter before work."

"Smart," she said. "You're so good about taking care of yourself. I need to be better at that."

"Don't worry, I'll remind you when I see you slacking," I teased.

"I'm sure you will." She laughed. "I'm still recovering from the laser hair removal you tricked me into trying."

"Ha, yes. That didn't go as well as I'd expected."

"I just want to make sure you're okay about last night. I'm sorry about what happened with Sebastian."

A few seabirds called overhead, swooping a few dozen feet before me in the sand, and I moved to the left. "Although I was pissed last night, I calmed down after a swim earlier." I snorted. "It's not like it's the first time there's been a fight in a club."

Nova hmphed. "True, but that's what's so odd about this whole thing. Diego, Sebastian, and Lucas bicker like brothers all day long, but they're not aggressive. He was out of character."

"Why do you think that happened?"

"I'm not sure. He said his wolf was confused by your scent."

"Ugh, not again." I groaned. "He was freaking me out about that last night. Wolf shifters and their damn sense of smell."

"And vampires, too. Apparently, Diego was so affected by my scent, he struggled against biting me."

"What?" I laughed. "Seriously?"

"Yep. I didn't know that until today."

"Well, I'm all set right now with any wolf shifters wanting to get with me because I smell like a yummy meal."

Nova sighed. "Sebastian stopped by earlier and apologized."

"It's fine," I replied.

"He wants to make it up to you. He offered to make dinner for all of us one night."

"That's *really* not necessary," I said.

"You sure? He's an amazing chef." Nova chuckled. "I wouldn't turn down a dinner when he's cooking."

"Yeah, it's fine. I'm able to feed myself." After that matter was resolved, I changed the subject. "What are you up to today?"

"Working on a project for the publisher and then some house stuff."

"How's the house coming along?"

Since moving from New York, she'd been gradually updating the place.

"Good. Thanks to you and the guys helping me. And you convincing me that I had to make the apartment my own has inspired me to refresh the look."

"You know I love to do that kind of stuff." I loved watching shows on redecorating and DIY projects and devoured magazines on the subject. A space needed personality and couldn't remain a blank canvas. You had to make it reflect your own style. Giving the Danger Zone its retro rock vibe had been tremendous fun. My staff and I had painted the walls black and added red and purple lights for ambiance. In addition, we put in all sorts of details picked up from old rock videos to give it a more signature look.

In my townhouse, I'd taken a different approach. It was my place to unwind, so it needed to be an oasis of comfort. That's why I'd picked more neutral tones and soft fabrics. When I was there, I wanted to relax.

"Is there anything you could use help with right now?" I asked her.

I'd convinced Nova that to truly feel like she lived in the house, she needed to make it her space. We had been tackling the belongings with a Marie Kondo attitude with me asking "Does it spark joy?" If not, it went bye-bye.

"Not sure," Nova said. "We finished painting the living room and moved the furniture back in. You're right about thinking I should get rid of it. I mean it's my aunt's style, and it doesn't really suit me, but I want to keep some things to remind me of her."

"Yet not a full museum," I reminded Nova.

"Exactly. I listened." She exhaled. "Do you want to come see it and give me some more pointers?"

Nova wasn't into decorating like I was. "I'm busy with the club tonight, but how about on Tuesday?"

"Ooh, that would be great," Nova replied. "We can order some food and hang out."

"And then have a total girl's night in. Watch a movie or something."

"That won't work since I don't have a TV," Nova reminded me. "Diego isn't working then, but I think the other guys are. I'm sure he won't mind if we watch a movie there."

"That's cool. I can tolerate hanging for a couple of hours with a vamp who helped saved my life and is now dating my best friend," I teased. The truth was I liked Diego, and Nova knew it. He could be grumpy, but he cared and would do anything for her—including risking his life.

A strange pang twisted inside. Would I ever find something like that? A connection with someone who'd be willing to sacrifice his life to save me?

Probably not. I'd never felt the urge to commit to anyone, which I attributed to my siren side. Why settle when I could be swimming among all those pretty fish in the sea?

SEBASTIAN

When Diego rolled zombie-like down the stairs late Monday morning, he said, "Hey, Seb. You're working tomorrow, right?"

I glanced up from the couch where I was scrolling my phone. "Yeah, why?"

"Gianna is going over to Nova's to help her with the apartment. When they're done, they might come by to watch a movie."

My wolf perked up, and my heartbeat quickened. Nova told me that Gianna turned down my offer for dinner and an apology, saying that things are fine between us, and I'd been contemplating my next course of action to meet up with her ever since.

"I suggested Monty Python, of course," Diego added with a shake of his head. "It baffles me that there are people who live in the twenty-first century who have never seen any of their stuff." He threw his hands up with dramatic flair and added, "What's wrong with people?"

"Gianna is coming here?"

"Only if you're not going to get all weird." Diego eyed me with wary speculation.

"I won't be," I scoffed with a casual wave. "Nova is your girl-friend. Gianna is her best friend. You and I are roommates, and

Nova is here all the time. It's normal for Gianna to come around."

Despite the forced calmness in my tone, my skin felt hot and clammy. My wolf clambered about inside.

"You sure about that?" Diego asked. "You're looking a little —bewildered."

"Bewildered?" I waved him off with a laugh. "You're misreading the situation. I'm totally cool with this."

He narrowed his eyes. "Why are you bouncing from one foot to the other like you can't sit still?"

"That's just my wolf," I explained. "We need to get out for a run."

Diego stared at me with a slow nod. "Yeah, you've been saying that."

Right. I'd worked last night, so I'd had to put it off. With the way my wolf was bounding about the prospect of seeing Gianna again, I needed to do something quick to avoid a repeat of the other night.

I glanced toward the kitchen. "Tell you what, I'll even make some appetizers for tomorrow."

He arched both brows. "Why? You're not even going to be here."

"It's just a small gesture to make amends for my earlier behavior. You know I love to cook."

And I sure the hell *would* be here tomorrow if Gianna was coming over. But I wouldn't let Diego know that as he might pull the plug on the plan.

CHAPTER 3

SEBASTIAN

It was close to midnight when I finished work. The best part of the night was when one of the chefs agreed to switch shifts, so I'd be there when Gianna came over.

I drove to a woodland reservation with plenty of space where I could let my wolf run free. After I found a secluded spot concealed by shadows to park, I entered the woods.

The moon loomed high and bright and would be full in a few more days. Snowfall from two nights ago still clung in patches, but the milder temperatures melted much of it.

I steered away from the path. I stayed off-trail to avoid anyone who might be out. The last thing a group of teens drinking in the woods wanted to see was a naked man wandering through the woods, and the last thing a shifter wanted was to be spotted by any humans who would freak out, so it was better to enter with stealth.

Once I ventured deeper into the woods on bare feet, sticking to the softer bedding of fern beneath evergreens rather than the patches of snow blanketing fallen leaves, I undressed and stashed my clothes and keys beneath the branches of a fallen tree.

I initiated the transformation. The vibrations rippled through my body, creating a strange combination of discomfort and pleasure. I didn't often shift, preferring to live in my human form, but with my wolf's restlessness in recent weeks, this was long overdue.

Once in wolf form, I padded beneath the dense woods up the hill, keeping my senses attuned for any nearby witnesses. When convinced that there were no humans nearby, I moved toward more open spaces. My wolf stretched beneath the moonlight.

Mate. He turned to run back and find Gianna.

No. Patience. I convinced him that if we behaved properly, we'd see her tomorrow.

With reluctance, my wolf relented and instead bounded up the hill. Able to run free, he sniffed at countless scents in the forest. We stopped at just about every patch of rodent, pine, scat, or urine. After catching a rabbit scent, he switched to hunting mode.

Hours later, we rested beneath the moon. Sleeping outside overnight was something I hadn't done in far too long.

When the first light of dawn spread through the branches over-head, I woke still in wolf form. Damn, I had to get out of here before any early morning hikers came out. I bounded down the hill toward my belongings and shifted to human form. Then I rushed to get dressed before leaving the concealment of the trees.

Once back in my car, I drove home. I crawled into bed, still exhausted from burning through all that energy last night.

When I woke a few hours later, a smile spread across my face. Gianna would be coming over later that day. Why her upcoming arrival excited me so was a surprise. After all, my wolf had burned through tons of energy last night. The restlessness should be gone.

Ah well, once he realized that Gianna was simply another woman and not one to go gaga for, that would change. Until then, I'd play the part of a good host and focus on preparations. I figured out the menu and went to the supermarket to pick up what I needed.

Lucas walked into the apartment that afternoon. "Why are you cooking up a storm? Thought you were working tonight."

"Plans have changed. Gianna is coming over with Nova later, and I want to make sure we are good hosts."

"Oh, shit." Lucas sighed. "Are you going to be cool?"

His gray cat, Shadow, bounced down the stairs and greeted Lucas by rubbing against his leg.

"Of course." I shrugged with nonchalance.

Lucas assessed me with a skeptical look before he bent down to greet Shadow with a chin rub.

"Cucumber cool," I added. "I let my wolf run last night. Don't worry, it's all good."

"Uh huh." Lucas's tone matched his expression.

"I have it all planned out," I said.

"What exactly?" He didn't look up as he moved on to rub Shadow's cheek.

Shadow reveled in the attention, purring with loud enthusiasm.

"Food brings everyone together."

Lucas laughed. "That's your answer to everything." He shook off some gray fur and then stood. "I have a better idea. Why don't you just sleep with her to get this out of your system?"

Hmm. I thought about it. That could work. It wasn't as if I hadn't thought about sleeping with her at least a dozen times already. If it had the bonus of helping to get her out of my head, even better.

Nope, my wolf dismissed immediately. *She's our mate.*

Still, it was worth a shot. I had to do something to be able to move on with my life. "Maybe."

Lucas chuckled. "It will be quite an accomplishment since she tossed you on your ass and then refused your invite to dinner."

I scowled. "I was off guard because of my wolf. I'm fine now." I raised my chin. "Tonight will be different. I'll be as smooth as butter sliding over hot, toasted Italian bread—and just as tasty."

Lucas laughed in doubt. "Twenty bucks says you fail. From what I've seen, Gianna is far from interested."

I shook his hand. "I won't fail."

Lucas grinned as he walked away. "Looks like I'll be headed to the record store tomorrow after you lose and pay up with a crisp twenty-dollar bill."

DIEGO WALKED IN AFTER SUNDOWN, carrying wine and beer. "Jeez, Sebastian. This looks like more than a few apps."

I'd cooked up a spread with a variety of appetizers, eager to impress. "I just made a few things to snack on." As I looked at the spread of glass-covered Pyrex covering the counter, I sensed I'd gone overboard. Then I dismissed it. It was better to have too much food than not enough.

"It's only going to be the three of us, and I barely eat."

"Four," I clarified. "I'll be here, too."

Sebastian clucked his tongue. "What about work?"

"Schedule change."

"Motherfucker," Diego joked with a shake of his head. "You definitely had a hand in that."

I tipped my head, admitting nothing.

Diego raised his index finger. "Don't be weird."

"Pshaw." I gestured with a dismissive wave. "Why is everyone so convinced that I can't act normal around Gianna?"

Diego pierced me with a knowing gaze. "Have you forgotten how you went all mad dog and attacked a stranger for touching her?"

I blinked. "Justified. He deserved it." I rolled my shoulders. "Besides, I finally went for a run in the woods. My wolf will be on his best behavior."

"Good." He pulled out his phone and texted. "I'm warning Nova in case they want to bail."

Fortunately, they didn't.

We played some video games over the next hour or so. I glanced in the direction of Nova's apartment several times. Was Gianna over there yet?

"You're full of shit," Diego declared when our game ended. He stared at me with an expression that called me out. "You can't stop looking over there."

Busted. "Okay, fine. I can't stop thinking about Gianna," I admitted. "What am I supposed to do about this?"

"If she's not interested, then you need to back off." Diego put his controller down on the coffee table.

I exhaled. "Great advice, man. Sooo helpful."

"What? It's the truth, right?"

"Not according to Lucas," I pointed out. "He thinks I should sleep with her, and that would get her out of my system."

"Then Lucas is an idiot," Diego said. "If she turned down your invitation for dinner, she's not going to want to sleep with you —even if you wormed your way into hanging out tonight."

That's exactly what I'd done. I adjusted my weight on the couch, searching for a more comfortable position. This siren was making me act out of character, and I didn't know how to deal with it.

"How did you convince Nova to give you a chance? It's not like you were suave with the creepy Nosferatu act when you first met." I snorted. "Not to mention tackling her to the ground."

"Yeah, point taken," Diego admitted with gritted teeth. "But that was entirely self-defense. Vampire plus sunlight leads to crispy body parts." He winced.

I tapped my foot on the area rug. "Since you are the master of awkward introductions and still managed to get the girl, what do you suggest I do?"

"I know nothing about being suave, as you already pointed out." He threw both hands in the air. "I guess my advice is—don't be a dick."

I blinked at him. "Your recommendation for me to get a stunning siren is—don't be a dick?"

"Yeah." He shrugged. "Be a decent guy."

"Legendary advice." My voice dripped with sarcasm as I rubbed my forehead. "You know, you should start your own dating podcast with those solid gems. You could call it 'Dating with Diego.' Or 'Diego's Dating Dos and Don'ts.' No, wait, we can milk the alliteration. How about "Don't be a Dick—Dating Dos and Don'ts with Diego.""

"Yeah, maybe I should," Diego agreed with faux seriousness. "I could dish advise here from home, not having to worry about waiting until sundown before I venture out to work."

His phone buzzed and he picked it up. "They're coming over now." He texted something back.

My pulse quickened, and I straightened my spine.

The door from Nova's apartment opened. When Gianna's voice reached me, I jumped up from the sofa.

Diego grabbed my arm and said, "Settle down, Seb," in a low tone.

"Right, right." I sat back on the couch, propping my head back onto my arm in a casual pose. It felt forced and unnatural. I shifted my position once more.

Diego stared at me. "Hey, squirm-io, are you good?"

"I'm fine," I said, my tone a higher pitch. Clearing my throat, I repeated, "Fine."

Diego blinked and shook his head as if this was a terrible mistake. Nova and Gianna walked into the living room a few seconds later.

Gianna raised two bottles of champagne, one in each hand. "Hey, hey! I brought some beverages."

The sight of the gorgeous woman with dark hair flowing over her shoulders and wearing skinny black jeans, an emerald-green shirt, and motorcycle boots made my heart thump. My wolf bounded with excitement declaring *mate*. I stood and stared at her, my tongue feeling like it had swelled to twice its size.

Diego stood. "Great, we'll have plenty. I stopped by the liquor store earlier." He took the bottles to the kitchen. "Champagne for you, Gianna?"

"You bet."

"Nova?"

"Sounds good."

Diego turned to me and arched his brows. "Sebastian?"

"Why not?" I replied with a smile. "It *is* a celebration, after all."

Everyone turned to stare at me in question.

"Celebration?" Nova furrowed her brows.

Shit, what was I talking about? Despite the excited shivers dancing about inside, I forced myself to calm down and come up with an excuse to cover up my nonsense. "It's the first time Gianna is hanging out with us here." My voice came out stran-gled. I cleared my throat and tipped my head to greet her. "Gianna."

"Hello, Sebastian." Amusement curled the edges of her lips, reaching up to her beautiful blue-violet eyes.

I almost swooned, lost, as my gaze locked on hers. To snap myself out of it, I attempted a lighthearted tone. "Welcome to our humble home." I bowed forward, but it rang as forced and out of place. "I hear a Monty Python viewing may be on the agenda—yet another reason for celebration." What the hell was I talking about, and why was my voice so deep? "Since I—uh—I heard you aren't familiar with it," I babbled, "I'm glad to be here as we pop your metaphorical cherry."

Nova grimaced and closed her eyes, and Diego cringed.

Gianna turned away as if shielding a laugh.

Pop. Her. Metaphorical. Cherry. In reference to watching Monty Python? Why did I say something like that? I pictured my head exploding, my brain erupting like confetti. Staying mute would have been better. I sounded like a combination of a pompous ass and uber nerd who had never spoken to a pretty woman before.

"Hell, yes, it will be a great night." Diego surprised me as he stepped forward and slapped me on the back. "Monty Python is always celebrated around here."

I silently thanked him for saving me from my increasing awkwardness. He could have held back and racked up the judgment points on dumb things to give me shit about in the morning. That would come, but at least it wouldn't happen in front of Gianna.

Why did words tumble out of my mouth without any sense of logic around her?

Time for me to move on to something I was more comfortable talking about, food. That might be the only way I could salvage my plan to woo Gianna before I stuck my big-ass paw into my big-ass mouth.

Again.

GIANNA

"I whipped up a couple of snacks." Sebastian motioned to the dining room table.

I glanced into the wood-paneled area where the table was covered with trays. "A few snacks? That looks more like a feast."

"I'm a chef, umm, so I tend to go overboard." He moved his weight from one foot to the other and avoided my gaze. "Better to have too much than too little."

He seemed nervous, but it was kind of sweet. "No complaints here. It smells delicious."

Nova had given me the heads up that Sebastian was home in case I wanted to cancel. I'd said it was fine. After all, we'd cross paths again, eventually.

"It's the least I can do after my behavior the other night." Sebastian hung his head. "I apologize. I was out of line."

"It's all right." I slanted my head. "What came over you? Are you usually that aggressive over a woman you just met?"

All sorts of emotions wrestled across his face. "No." He exhaled. "My wolf was restless and acted up. We went out for a long run. All good now."

I clucked my tongue. "O-kay. Just don't do it again. I can't have brawls at my business." I arched my brows. "Especially if it brings attention to supernaturals causing trouble. Know what I mean?"

He had a hangdog expression. "I do. And I promise that it won't happen again." He raised his gaze to meet mine. "Are we cool?"

"We're cool," I replied with an easygoing smile. "It's easier that way—since my best friend is dating your roommate. We're bound to run into each other. No point in being salty, right?"

"Right." He smiled. "Can I get you a drink?"

"I think Diego is pouring the champagne." I turned toward the kitchen where Diego was pulling out the cork and Nova was getting flutes.

He shook his head, "Right. Right. We went over that." He ran his hand through his rich, dark hair as if flustered.

The pop of the champagne cork followed, and we turned to Diego.

After we all had a glass, Nova raised hers. "To friendships, new and old."

"Here here," I saluted and clinked their glasses. Then I sipped the chilled champagne.

"I'd like that." Sebastian glanced at me before drinking some of his.

He put his glass down on an end table and walked over to the food. "How about a plate?" He offered me one.

"Thanks." I stepped over to accept it and examined the options. "What do we have here?"

"This is a gruyere cheese and crab palmier," he pointed out. "That has figs, goat cheese, and prosciutto. And that's bacon-wrapped scallops with a hint of maple syrup."

"Ooh, interesting."

"That's a honey-mint lamb skewer. And there's some smoked salmon." As Sebastian introduced each dish, his confidence seemed to return.

"Looking forward to trying them," I said. "I hear you're an excellent chef."

A proud smile spread across his face. "Thank you."

Sebastian smelled good, freshly showered, and he was kind of cute. He had kind eyes that were beautiful shades of brown, honey-colored in the center and darker at the outer circle. If we hadn't had that debacle at the club, things could have ended up quite differently that night.

No, it was better that we didn't get involved at all. After all, like Nova said, with our mutual friendships, we'd likely run into each other again.

Once my plate was overflowing, he welcomed me into the living room. It had high ceilings, maroon oriental carpeting, a record player with a case of records, and a flat-screen TV.

I sat on the brown suede sofa and glanced around. "It's a great place you have here." I took a bite of the bacon-wrapped scallops "Mmm, this is delicious. Well done, Sebastian."

He gestured with a casual wave. "It was nothing. You should come by the restaurant."

"Maybe," I replied in a noncommittal tone.

Nova sat beside me on the sofa with Diego next to her. Sebastian sat on the recliner. We chatted and drank and sampled the delicious appetizers.

After we'd finished our first glasses and had refills, Nova asked, "We ready for a movie?"

I shrugged. "Sure."

"After all, it's a Monty Python celebration," she teased, grinning at Sebastian.

"*Life of Brian?*" Diego suggested.

"A classic," Sebastian noted.

"I haven't seen that one," Nova said.

I shrugged. "Let's do it."

A few minutes later, I was introduced to the strange world with its bizarre animation sequence and lyrics. Soon, I laughed with them at the ridiculousness on the screen.

"What is this farcical nonsense?" I asked.

"Genius farcical nonsense," Diego corrected with a thumbs up and clicking sound.

We ate and drank throughout the movie.

At the end, Sebastian and Diego sang along to "Always Look on the Bright Side of Life" while Nova and I chuckled.

Once the credits rolled, I stood. "I'm going to get going."

Sebastian jumped to his feet. "I can walk you out."

"That's not necessary. My car is right in the driveway." I pointed outside.

His expression turned down. "Oh."

A twinge of sympathy rose. He'd been considerate in preparing all this food, and we'd had a good time hanging out watching the movie. "Everything was delicious, Sebastian. Thanks."

He perked up again. "Glad you liked it. Once again, I'm sorry about the other night."

"Apology accepted." I smiled. "Tell you what, we're having a New Year's Eve party at the club next week. If you're not doing anything—and able to keep your hands to yourself," I added with a grin. "You and Lucas should come."

His eyes brightened, and he nodded. "I'll be there."

After I thanked them for having me and said goodnight, Nova walked with me outside.

"I hope it wasn't too weird with Sebastian," she said. "I've never seen him act this way around anyone. He must have a little crush on you."

"It's fine. It was harmless." I quirked a smile.

"I'm surprised you invited him back to the club."

"He's been trying so hard to make up for it, I can't hold it against him forever." I shrugged one shoulder. "Besides, he's kind of cute."

"Really? You think so?"

"Don't worry, I'm not going to hook up with him."

"What?" Nova blinked in surprise. "I didn't say anything about that."

"I'm just saying—he's kind of hot. If it was a one-night thing, I wouldn't mind giving it a go." That was another thing I attributed to my siren side—my hearty libido. I pushed some hair behind my ears. "But we may cross paths often through you and Diego, so it's not a good idea. And since I've already seen his possessive side, that's a hell no."

SEBASTIAN

The days counting down until New Year's Eve stretched on as the longest of the year, yet I had to be patient. Gianna had invited me back to her club, and I wouldn't blow it this time.

When I walked into the Danger Zone with Lucas, Diego, and Nova, my hands turned clammy.

Diego and Nova walked ahead, arm in arm. I was still surprised to see him with anyone. He'd been a reclusive vampire ever since we'd met. His vampire lover had turned him and stopped his heart before breaking it. I didn't blame him for being wary, but how long could a guy brood at home? Fortunately, Nova came along and smacked some life back into his dead heart.

Whitesnake's "Still of the Night" played as we entered, the sound echoing around us.

Sensing she was close, my wolf tensed and took notice. I shook out my limbs.

Lucas leaned over. "Are you good?"

"Peachy." I'd taken my wolf out every night this week to burn through his agitation. I had to. Ever since Gianna had left our house, I'd been consumed by the promise of seeing her tonight. My wolf hadn't realized the error of confusing her as our mate. In fact, he was more insistent than ever.

"What happened the last time I was here will not happen again," I promised. "Tonight, I will be smooth as your waxed chest, my friend."

Lucas chuckled. An exotic dancer, he often spent more time manscaping than I did to get himself in prime visual form before he went to dance on stage for the ladies. Then again, a dragon shifter wasn't cursed with as much hair as a wolf, so aside from his long blond hair, he probably didn't have as much to deal with.

"Shall we put some money on you getting kicked out again?" Lucas proposed.

"I don't think so." I'd already lost twenty bucks to him the last time I'd seen her.

Tonight, something felt different. I could sense it.

How? I wasn't sure. When it came to Gianna, nothing went as I'd planned. She'd been tough on my ass the first time, which had been well deserved. But at my house, she'd been more relaxed and casual. The four of us hanging out had been fun despite my verbal incontinence—as well as having to ward off a mega boner with her so close to me.

The club was so packed with people wearing sparkly tiaras, New Year's hats, and other gaudy gear that would be trashed after midnight. Diego and Nova had entered right before us and were quickly swallowed by the crowd. How would I ever find Gianna?

"Bar?" Lucas suggested.

"Yup." We headed that way and had to wait through a couple of songs before it was our turn.

I ordered the Moscow Mule drink I'd had last time and the gin and tonic one again for Lucas. Although I searched for any signs of Gianna, from her face in the crowd to her alluring scent to the sound of her voice, she remained elusive. The club was too crowded for me to get a good sense of her location.

Maybe she wasn't here tonight.

That would ruin everything. Still, I had to make the best of it. It was a New Year's Eve party, and I was celebrating with my friends.

Lucas insisted we dance. I went along with the idea, although half-hearted at first, I was determined to try to have a good time. We found a spot in a group of women who hooted and hollered with the music that played lively songs from the 80s and 90s.

When we were ready for a break, we headed back to the bar. That's where I spotted Gianna. My mouth went dry.

Mate. My wolf whimpered, pushing me to get closer.

Not yet, I insisted. If we wanted any chance with her, we had to remain calm. I couldn't bumble all over myself again, erupting nonsense in a vomit of word soup.

My pulse quickened and my body felt hot. *Act casual.*

Midnight was coming up and with it, the countdown. If I could get close to Gianna before the midnight kiss, I could nonchalantly suggest it. That meant beating out any other men who wanted the same thing. My wolf stirred and grumbled.

If I wanted the chance of a midnight kiss, that meant no more prowling and growling. The plan wasn't foolproof, but it was the only one I had.

GIANNA

Business was hot tonight. I checked on the bartenders, the bar backs, the bouncers, and the rest of the staff to make sure the night was running smoothly. All went well.

The cash registers were filling up. It was time for mama to have a little fun. I took my champagne cocktail and wandered through the club, checking out the eye candy.

As I moved along the edges of the club, I spotted Nova and Diego dancing to Madonna's "Vogue," part of the upbeat playlist for the party tonight. Seeing who Nova had initially described as a grumpy vampire frame his face in the Vogue move was a sight. I chuckled as I approached through the crowd and hip-checked her to say hello.

"Glad you both came," I shouted over the music.

"Me, too," she replied.

"Thanks for the invite," Diego said.

"You've got some moves, vamp," I teased, mimicking the Vogue move he'd just done.

He planted his hand on one hip and flashed a serious look. "Strike a pose."

Nova and I laughed.

"Looks like Blue Steel," I noted the Derek Zoolander reference.

He moved his hand on the other hip. "How's this one? I call it Magnum."

We laughed and then danced some more.

After the song ended, I asked, "Did Sebastian and Lucas come?"

"They're around somewhere," Nova motioned.

I nodded, searching the general area. "I'm going to walk around," I said, letting them enjoy themselves.

As I made my way through the crowd and back toward the bar, a striking woman wearing a long black trench coat strode my way. She was even taller than me and sashayed over with a sultry walk and Mona Lisa smile that captured the attention of everyone she passed. Who was this woman and why was her gaze fixed on me? She looked familiar somehow, but I would have remembered her had we met.

As she approached, she smiled. "You must be Gianna."

I furrowed my brows. "Can I help you?"

"Yes." She inclined her head. "I'm here to see you."

Something about this woman was disconcerting despite the smile. I tried to get a better read on her. She was maybe a decade or two older than me but had an ageless way about her. "Do I know you?"

She nodded. "We met a long, long time ago. You wouldn't remember."

Although I was intrigued, this was getting a bit irksome. "Okay, so who are you?"

She outstretched her arms to her sides. "I'm your mother."

My heart shot up to the rafters. My—*mother*? Why would she come here, now—if she was even who she said she was?

"How—what…" I stammered. "How do I know you're telling the truth?"

She pushed her hair over her shoulders and then lowered her arms. "The physical resemblance isn't enough?" She grinned. "You look just like me."

My mouth opened and closed like a fish. My mother just walked into my life for the first time in twenty-five years. The same woman who'd abandoned me when I was an infant.

Confusing emotions swirled in me like in a whirlpool. Who the hell was she to just barge in after all this time?

My hands trembled. "Where have you been my entire life?"

She pouted. "Oh, Gianna. I can understand that you'd be upset, but our ways aren't the ways of humans."

"Oh, really?" I summoned up sarcasm while my resentment simmered into a low, boiling rage. "Do tell."

She gestured with a dismissive wave. "We don't live that way with a house, two kids, two cars, and all that nonsense."

"I wouldn't know," I drawled with contempt and crossed my arms. "Because you weren't around to tell me."

She lowered her chin. "I'm here now. I'd like to get to know you."

I stared at her, wary of this woman who was blood and yet a stranger. Then again, she was my mother, and she had the answer to the giant question that haunted me my entire life—why?

"I'll think about it."

"I know this is a surprise. How about I call you in a couple of days after it settles in?"

As she walked away, heads turned. My gaze was glued to her back.

My hands shook. I needed a drink. Pronto. Although there was a line of people waiting, one of my bartenders, Kylie, poured me a shot of vodka. As soon as I swallowed and put the shot glass on the bar, Sebastian stepped beside me.

"Gianna, are you okay? You're shaking."

"No." I shook my head and stared into his eyes. So warm and full of concern.

"What's wrong?" His voice was gentle. "How can I help you?"

What I needed right now was a distraction. I couldn't let all my simmering resentment at my mother's abandonment and her surprise arrival rise and swallow me.

My go to was with sensual diversion.

"Take me home with you." I grabbed his bicep. "Now."

CHAPTER 4

SEBASTIAN

I blinked at Gianna. No way had I just heard what I thought I did. "Now?" I echoed. "It's not even midnight."

"I don't care." She wrapped one arm around herself. "I want to get out of here."

Whoever that woman was talking to Gianna had upset her. With their resemblance, I guessed they were related.

"What happened?" I asked her.

She closed her eyes and then reopened them, fixing a hard stare on me. "I don't want to talk about it right now."

"Okay."

She drummed her fingers on her hip. "Do you want to leave with me, or should I find someone else?"

Fuck. No.

Time to get my head out of my ass. "Let's go." Putting my hand on her lower back, I steered her toward the exit. "Do you have a coat?" I'd left mine in the car, but then again, the cold didn't bother me much.

"It's in my office," she replied. "Be right back."

When she walked away, I texted Lucas and Diego. *I'm leaving with Gianna. Find another way home.*

I'd driven us all. Since we were all supernatural, alcohol didn't affect us like it did humans, and I already felt stone-cold sober. Then again, if I hadn't, Gianna's invitation would have woken any man up from the grave.

You dog, Lucas texted. *Don't worry, I'm not planning on coming home tonight.*

Diego wrote, *Don't mess this up.*

What he meant could refer to many things, but most likely had to do with Gianna being Nova's best friend. If I was a dick, it would have collateral damage on his relationship.

The music faded out and the DJ spoke about the countdown coming up. Funny, this had been my original plan to get in Gianna's orbit before the countdown and now she was nowhere in sight. Hopefully, she hadn't changed her mind.

The DJ started the countdown, and everyone joined in. "10... 9... 8..."

I paced near the entrance. Where was Gianna?

"7... 6... 5..."

She's going to bail on me, isn't she?

"4... 3..."

I would stand here by myself at the start of a new year. Alone. My gut sank.

"2... 1..."

"Happy New Year!"

"Happy New Year, Sebastian."

I turned at the sound of the woman's voice behind me while most of the people nearby embraced. "Gianna."

She had her coat on and a bright smile. She stepped closer and put her hand on my cheek. As she leaned closer, the noise of the club faded, and my heartbeat drummed louder, echoing in my head. Time slowed as her scent filled my nostrils, imbuing me with a heady burst of need.

And then her lips touched mine. An electric buzz heated my blood.

Mate, my wolf murmured in contentment.

She pulled away and stared at me with a dazed expression. That's how I felt—confused about the magical swells rippling inside. Did she feel it, too?

Her lips parted. "Did you bring a car?"

It took me a couple of seconds to process the question. "Yes."

"Let's go." She looped her arm through mine.

As we walked toward the exit, many men stared. They'd probably kill to exchange places with me. It didn't bother me as I rode the high from our brief, but definitely not last, kiss of the night.

GIANNA

During the drive back to Salem, Sebastian asked me once more if something was wrong. I shut that conversation down quickly. The last thing I wanted to do was talk about the unexpected and shattering arrival of the woman who'd abandoned me.

Instead, I deflected conversation and turned the music up. We didn't speak much during the drive, and I tried not to slip deeper into the turmoil churning in my brain.

Once we entered his house, he asked, "Do you want a drink? Or something to eat?"

His penchant to want to feed me was charming. And he smelled delicious. His masculine scent had an edge of wildness to it I couldn't explain, but it must have been part of his wolf side.

"No, I only want you." I stepped closer to him. What I needed was a distraction, preferably a sensual one.

Hunger burned hot and bright in his eyes. "Gianna..." he rumbled.

I wrapped one hand around the back of his head, ruffling my fingers through his thick, dark hair. "Do you want me, Sebastian?"

"So much..." His voice was low and husky.

"Then shut up and kiss me." I leaned in and pressed my lips to his.

That dizzying sensation from our brief kiss from earlier returned. What was it? I could only describe it as enchanting.

It must have been his wolf magic. It didn't matter. All I wanted was to purge myself of the shit feeling. My mother's arrival unearthed too many painful memories. I yearned to smother them, to feel wanted and desired. This growly, somewhat awkward wolf with the small crush on me was the perfect one to fill that void tonight.

He wrapped his arms around me and claimed my mouth with desperate possessiveness. Yes, this was what I needed. He kissed me deep and hard until we were both panting.

Then he threw me over his shoulder, and I squealed in surprise. "What are you doing?"

"Taking you to my bed."

"Yes." Heat uncurled in my core.

All his awkward bumbling from our earlier encounters disappeared as he took control, a total turn on. He carried me up the stairs without showing any exertion.

Once in his room, I quickly noted the royal blue walls and dark furniture and how tidy everything was arranged. He captured me in a heated kiss again and led me to his bed, which was covered with a soft, blue plaid comforter. He pulled it down, revealing high-quality, light-blue sheets. This shifter was neat and had good taste.

Sebastian ran his large, possessive hands over my body. He followed with his mouth, kissing me from my face to down over my dress, covering my breasts and then my torso. When he slid his hands beneath my dress, stroking up my leg, I gasped with greater need.

"Take it off," I begged, sitting up to pull off my dress.

He aided with unzipping it and sliding it over my head. When he removed my heeled boots, he kissed my lower leg. Hell, his mouth felt good on me. I wanted more.

We scrambled to remove my remaining clothes, the black stockings, satin bra, and panties.

Sebastian's eyes sparkled with a golden hunger as his gaze caressed my body and he murmured, "You're fuckin' gorgeous, Gianna."

I was also completely naked on his bed while he was fully dressed. "I want to see you."

Reaching for him, I pulled his navy-blue shirt out of his pants and fumbled to unbutton it. He removed his shirt and unfastened his pants. Ooh, this shifter was impressive. He took care of himself. My favorite partner was one who took care of his body as well as mine. My fingers itched to touch his muscles and caress every cut in his core.

"I like what I see," I crooned.

As he grinned with pride, I stroked from his shoulder down his toned torso. I pulled him on top of me. While we kissed, I reached down and cupped his ass. It was as tight and firm as the rest of him. He pressed his hard length against my thigh. I moaned. So promising.

I tugged his pants down his hips, desperate to feel him inside me—and soon.

SEBASTIAN

Gianna was a goddess—beautiful, sensual, and—

Our mate, my wolf insisted.

With the way she captivated my senses, I couldn't deny we had some sort of connection.

She gazed at me from under fringed lashes. Her dark hair with red streaks splayed across my pillowcase. My gaze roamed over her luscious, naked curves. While I undressed, the deprivation of her touch spurred me to tear off my clothes in record time.

Finally free of them, I crawled back over the beauty in my bed. Gianna released a soft moan and pulled my body against hers. I kissed her, practically plundering her mouth in my desperate need for her. Then I slid down her body, touching her soft skin. I cupped her full breasts, taking each tight nipple into my mouth, and she arched up.

"Oh, yes, that feels so good," she murmured.

Although I could savor her breasts this way all night long, I needed to touch and taste all of her. I kissed and licked down her torso and then moved to the inside of her thighs. The scent of Gianna's desire left me throbbing with an ache to bury myself deep inside her. But not yet—not until she shuddered with pleasure.

I swirled my tongue up her inner thighs, teasing her, and she reached up, grasping my shoulders and begging for more. Yes, just like that.

I finally gave in to what we both craved, tasting her with a long, slow caress. She released a low sigh.

She tasted intoxicating, more exquisite than any dish I'd ever created. She ran her hands through my hair and sighed in pleasure.

I yearned to lose myself with this addictive siren.

"Oh, Sebastian." The raspy sound of my name from her mouth was the most sensual thing I'd ever heard.

My desire ramped up with hers until we were both mad with desire. When I brought her to her peak, she cried out in passion, such a captivating sound. Trembling beneath me, she arched her beautiful body into a bow before falling back onto the bed.

I slid over her and rubbed my aching erection in between her legs. "You taste so good. I could feast on you all night."

A sensual smile spread across her face, still marked by rapture. "Ooh, I'd like that, wolf." She reached between my legs and stroked my hard length. "But I want this more right now."

Although drugged by raw need, a question rose through. "Should I wear a condom?"

"No, I'm protected." She pulled me closer.

Supes weren't susceptible to human diseases so as long as we had the pregnancy aspect covered, we were good.

"I want to feel every inch of you." When I slid the tip in, the incredible tightness dizzied me.

"Yes, Sebastian," she cried and wrapped her legs around me. "I need you."

I drove in slowly, letting her adjust to my presence. "You feel amazing."

Finally, I was fully inside. I paused, enthralled by how right this felt. As I moved in and out, the urgency to thrust harder grew. My canines pierced my gums, itching with a yearning he'd never felt before—to bite this woman and claim her as my mate.

Fuck. I froze. That concept was terrifying—thrilling and terrifying.

"Something wrong?" Gianna asked.

"No, everything is perfect. You're so hot, I need a moment." That part was true. I needed to regroup before I lost control. "Turn around," I directed, my voice a growly command.

She moved onto her hands and knees, pushing out her beautiful ass and then peered over her shoulder with a seductive glance.

I drove back inside her and gripped her hips. As I pumped harder and faster, her moans grew louder. Heat consumed me, smoldering beneath my skin. I was breathing hard, hovering on the edge, but no way would I come without taking care of her again.

Reaching around, I slid my fingers in between her legs and found her sensitive nub. I added more pressure as I circled it and thrust harder.

Gianna grasped the pillow. "Yes, fuck me just like this, wolf."

Hell, yes. The headboard slammed into the wall over and over. Fortunately, we were alone because I couldn't hold back.

"Come for me," I hissed.

She tightened around me and cried, "Yes, Sebastian."

As she pulsed around my shaft, I lost the final shard of control. Intense pressure thundered through my veins. The urge to bite and claim her almost overpowered me, but I held on, almost passing out.

I dropped my head back and released a growl that vibrated from deep within my chest as I exploded deep inside her.

Completely spent, I rolled onto my back, and she did the same. Our loud breathing echoed around us.

"That was just what I needed tonight," she said.

Right. This was just desire. She wanted me for one night, just as I wanted her for the same. Maybe now my wolf would abandon the ridiculous notion that we were mates.

My already rapid heart hammered even faster, but for a different reason—fear.

Because I sensed that wouldn't happen. I *knew* it wouldn't.

The impulse to claim her pounded through me with more urgency than ever. I started to see that what my wolf had been drumming into my head might be possible.

Gianna, this siren who didn't want to be chained by any relationship was the one.

She was my mate.

CHAPTER 5

GIANNA

When I woke up, spooned by a man with a muscular arm and glanced around the room with shades of blue, I remembered where I was.

Shit. Maybe last night was a bad idea. The sex was great, but since I was upset by my mother's unexpected appearance, I hadn't been thinking straight. I definitely hadn't thought through any repercussions. Would there be any? Sebastian could be awkward, but he was also sweet.

As long as I kept him straight that this was a one-night thing, we could move on without any complications.

When Sebastian stirred, pressing his erection against me, eager for another round, I struggled against jumping back on that party train.

I wiggled away and climbed out of bed, searching for my discarded clothes. "Last night was fun."

"This morning could be, too," he suggested.

The way his gaze traveled over me ignited the heat once more, but I had to get my head straight. My mother's arrival had opened a can of squirmy red wigglers, and I had yet to process it.

"Sorry, but it won't be happening again."

"Why not?" Sebastian sat up.

I stared at his muscular torso, struggling against the urge to run my tongue over the dips leading down...

"Because this can't go anywhere." I motioned between us. "I'm not interested in dating or any form of a relationship. I don't know why anyone settles for mundane monogamy." When I found my bra and panties, I put them on. The stockings I rolled into a ball. No way was I dealing with sliding those babies on right now.

"Oh, I'll find a way to keep things interesting and far from routine," he proposed with a devilish grin.

My awareness was drawn to my lady parts. No, I couldn't encourage this. Grabbing my dress off the floor, I slid it over my head and down my body. "I need to go."

Sebastian stood, stark naked and fully erect. "Let me make you breakfast first."

I avoided drooling over his promising thick length. "What are you going to do with that thing? Use it as a spatula?"

He chuckled. "We can experiment with it however you'd like."

I bit my lip. Damn, that offer was tempting.

"What would you like?" Sebastian asked. "An omelet, pancakes? I have it all." He pulled on some boxer shorts.

Breakfast did sound good. I was hungry after last night, and Sebastian was a good cook.

He had roommates, though, and I didn't want to face any awkward conversations in the kitchen. I should have asked him to come to my place instead. In my urgency to escape, I really hadn't thought things through.

"Pancakes," I replied. "If we can avoid any conversations with your roommates."

Sebastian pulled on a pair of blue flannel lounge pants and then arched a brow. "Are you ashamed of being here with me?" he teased.

"I don't want to deal with any speculation this morning."

"Got it." He pulled out his phone.

"What are you doing?"

"Texting Lucas. He said he wasn't coming home last night. I want to make sure. If Diego is even here, he'll be sleeping until late morning."

Once he confirmed that we had the place to ourselves, I used the bathroom to freshen up, and Sebastian went downstairs to start breakfast.

The scent of cooking bacon wafted up the stairs and my mouth watered.

Several minutes later, I sat across from him at the dining room table, lamenting that he was now dressed as I would have enjoyed the view. He'd piled pancakes, eggs, bacon, and sliced bananas onto plates for each of us and poured us each a mug of steaming coffee.

Staying for breakfast was a good idea. Perhaps I should have taken him up on starting the day with another round in bed.

While I chewed some scrambled eggs, I thought about my mother. Was I even ready to talk to her yet?

"What's wrong?" Sebastian asked. "You prefer your eggs a different way?"

"No, they're delicious." I exhaled. "It's just something on my mind."

"Like last night." He nodded with a sage expression. "It was that woman, right?"

I recoiled. "You saw her?"

"I was nearby and saw how she upset you. When she walked away, that's when I came to see if you were all right."

And I'd pretty much jumped his bones. Or more like his muscular body since this burly shifter didn't have a bony angle on him. I sighed. Again. One more time and I could be crowned the queen of drama.

"Yes, she's the reason I was disturbed," I admitted.

"Who is she?"

I grunted. Was that a step up from another sigh? "My long-lost mother."

His eyes widened. "What do you mean by long-lost? She hasn't been part of your life?"

"I'm not going to tell you my personal problems." I took a bite of pancakes dripping with Vermont maple syrup.

"Why not? Does telling me make them worse?" He ate some bacon, devouring almost half the strip in one bite.

"No, but—I barely know you."

"That makes me impartial—and a good sounding board, right?"

I sized him up. What guy wanted to listen to a woman talk through what's on her mind? Oh well, he asked for it, so he'd hear it all—and then probably regret his question.

I spilled the situation with my mother out in a rambling speech, finishing with, "Who does she think she is? She's never been a part of my life, and then she shows up out of nowhere, on New Year's Eve of all times, after twenty-five years? What kind of bullshit is that?"

"That is big," Sebastian noted. He'd stopped eating as he'd listened to my tale.

"Does she really think I'm going to welcome her back into my life after she abandoned me?"

He cocked his head, appearing to think about the options. "What do you think you'll do?"

"I don't know." I stabbed some more pancakes and eggs together and scooped them into my mouth. After I ate, I said, "I need to talk to Nova."

After we finished eating and brought our plates into the kitchen, I texted Nova.

Are you home?

Yes, she replied.

Can I come over for a few?

Sure.

I'll be right there.

When I walked over to the door leading into her apartment, Sebastian followed me and said, "I want to see you again."

"I don't think so. It's not a good idea."

"Why not? I think it's a great idea. Think about it some more."

"I told you it's not my style. I'm not girlfriend material."

"Good, I'm not looking for a girlfriend. We had a good time together. Why not meet up again?"

"Sebastian…" Another sigh. Where was my damn drama queen crown?

"We had a sizzling connection last night; one we shouldn't ignore. Something my wolf recognized the—"

He stopped and turned ghostly pale.

"What?"

"Nothing."

"No, it *definitely* is something." I crossed my arms. "Tell me what you were about to say."

He rubbed the side of his face. "The reason my wolf acted up the first time we met was…"

When he didn't finish, I prodded, "Sebastian?"

He exhaled with a whoosh. "He thought you were our mate."

I stared at him and then I laughed. "Good one." I raised my index finger. "You look so serious, you almost had me there."

"It's true," he insisted, fixing an earnest gaze on me. "That's why I acted so weird."

I assessed him. "Are you crazy?"

He rolled a shoulder and frowned. "It feels like it lately."

"Oh, I should have known better than to think this," she paused to motion between us, "was a good idea."

"It *was* a great idea." His eyes widened.

"I'm no one's mate," I protested. "That's ridiculous." I'd planned on cutting over to Nova's apartment from their shared kitchen, but I needed to get some air. I headed to his front door. "Thanks for breakfast, but I'm out."

He followed me. "I want to see you again, Gianna."

"That is *not* going to happen."

"Why not? Didn't you enjoy yourself?"

I did. "Yeah, but that doesn't mean I'm going to get hitched up with you after you reveal *that* nonsense."

His expression contorted as he appeared to struggle with something. "Don't worry, I don't believe that mate thing. It was just my wolf confused and acting all frisky. After I let him out to run, he settled down."

I eyed him. "Are you sure?"

"Yes." He glanced away. "I'm on board with what you want."

"And what's that?"

"A good time. Nothing serious." He shrugged.

I opened the front door. "I'm not interested in getting involved with anyone, Sebastian. Bye."

Once I closed it behind me, I exhaled. What did I get myself into? Crazy wolf.

After a few deep breaths, I walked over to Nova's side and knocked.

She opened the door. "That was quick. Were you in the neighborhood?"

"Indeed." I gave her a sheepish grin as I pointed my thumb to the right. "Next door."

Her eyes widened. "Diego said you left with Sebastian. I didn't think…" She blinked. "Really? You and him?"

I clucked my tongue, ignoring the question. "Is Diego here?"

"No, he went back to his room to get more sleep. I get up much earlier than a vampire."

I nodded, grateful we hadn't crossed paths.

Nova lifted her mug as she headed to her sofa. "Do you want some coffee?"

"No, I had plenty." Sebastian ensured my appetite was satiated in more ways than one. "I need to tell you what happened last night." I sat down beside her. "My mother showed up at the club."

Nova's eyes bugged out. "Your *mother*?"

"Exactly."

Nova knew how epic this arrival was, so I didn't have to explain.

"Why would she seek you out last night after all these years?"

"She said she wants to get to know me. What am I supposed to think?"

Nova blew out with a whoosh. "It's—wow—I can't even imagine. What did you say?"

"I said I'd think about it."

"Wicked bats and flying monkeys. Are you going to tell your dad?"

Yikes. That was something I'd have to think about. "I don't know. He'd definitely have some strong feelings on the matter." After all, she'd walked out, leaving him to raise an infant on his own. "I'm probably better off not telling him. Yet."

"Yeah, that's a good idea," Nova said with a nervous laugh. "Your dad can be scary when he's pissed off."

"Ugh, don't I know it." I dropped my head back. Despite his master level at intimidation, I'd learned to stand up to him at some point in my rebellious teenage years.

Glancing in the direction of Sebastian's apartment, I said, "After my mother left the club, I freaked. All these crazy emotions raged through me, and I desperately wanted to shut them down. When Sebastian came to check on me, I practically demanded he take me home." With a sheepish grin, I added, "Sorry if that adds any awkwardness to your living situation."

She brushed it off with a wave. "Please, we're all adults." She touched her temples. "Oh man, was he super weird?"

More like incredible in bed. "He was fine."

"Does this mean you and him?" Nova made a circular gesture to complete the sentence.

"No," I dismissed. "It was just a one-night thing. I needed a distraction. He was there, willing and able. That's all there is to it."

"Got it."

It was a great night despite my emotional turmoil with my mother. And breakfast with him this morning wasn't that bad either. But then, there was that disturbing revelation this morning.

"It might have been a bad idea," I added.

"Why?"

I pursed my lips. "He said his wolf thought I was his mate."

"Ah, shit." Nova crossed her legs. "Minor complication," she added in a wry tone.

"He thinks it was a mix-up. His wolf was confused by my scent or something."

"Ah, yes, that's what he told me."

"He told you?" I asked. "What else did he say?"

"That was pretty much it," Nova replied.

"He's so freakin' strange." I slapped my hands on my thighs. "And that's why it will only be one-night. It *won't* be happening again."

SEBASTIAN

Go back to her, my wolf insisted. *She's right next door.*

What for? Gianna had made her feelings clear. She was not interested in any sort of relationship, or even hooking up, ever again.

Whatever connection I'd felt last night, I'd have to ignore until it went away. What was the point of pining after someone you could never have?

I'd have to find a way to tear her out of my head. I had to be strong enough to resist my wolf's urges because this siren wouldn't be singing any song to lure me back to her.

AT LUNCH TIME, I was making a roast beef sandwich with all the fixings when Lucas entered the house.

"Hey, how was your night?" I asked.

"Amazing." He nodded wide a wide smile. "I went home with a beauty. Hot damn, that's a great club. Plenty of hot, single women wanting to play. I'm definitely going back."

While Lucas continued with the highlights, my mind wandered back to Gianna's situation. Why would her mother abandon Gianna and then come back into her life after so many years? No wonder she was distressed.

"Sebastian, you with me?" Lucas grabbed a pickle spear from the open jar on the counter and took a bite.

Snapping me out of my thoughts, I answered, "Yeah, why?"

"I asked you a question, but you were off in la-la land." He pointed down at my sandwich. "You've been spreading mayo on that bread long enough for it to pass through to the other side."

I blinked and put the knife down. This wasn't like me. Lucas and I loved to share stories of our conquests. But instead of sharing mine, I admitted, "I'm a little rattled."

"About what?"

"I was with Gianna last night."

"Nice." He nodded with approval.

I exhaled. "I thought one night would get this compulsion out of my system. No dice. Not yet at least."

Lucas pulled out a plate and placed two slices of the whole wheat bread on it. "What do you mean—you want to be with her again?"

"Worse." I grunted. "I sense what my wolf has been telling me might be true—that Gianna is my mate."

"Eek." Lucas put his fingers in the sign of a cross and backed up as if warding off a vampire in the movies.

"It's not a death sentence."

"It might as well be," he scoffed. "You need an exorcism or something to get rid of that shit. It's a curse."

"You know, you're part shifter, too," I noted. "This could happen to you one day."

"Oh, hell no." He squeezed some mustard onto his bread. "I'll fly away before I let some mate curse bind me."

I exhaled. "I don't know what to do. She doesn't want it. I don't want it. You're right, it does seem like a curse."

"Sorry about that, man. If neither of you wants it, it's bound to fade away, right?"

The cat sauntered into the kitchen. "Hey Shadow, want a treat?" Lucas pulled out the bag of treats and tossed a few. Then he finished piling roast beef, tomato, and lettuce onto his sandwich, closed it, and took a massive bite.

Although I'd been going through the motions of making my own lunch, I didn't have an appetite—an absolute rarity. "I hope you're right and that in a day or two, I'll be back to my normal self."

"Fingers crossed, man," Lucas declared. "I mean, she's hot, but no woman is worth that stranglehold that comes with being chained to a mate for life."

"You don't have to tell me that." I rolled my shoulders. "I just need to shake it off."

Lucas shook his hips and sang Taylor Swift's song of the same name.

I laughed. The break in the tension that had imprisoned me lately took some weight off my shoulders.

Diego descended the stairs that moment and blinked at us from sleepy eyes. He groaned. "I've woken up in vampire purgatory."

Lucas bumped Diego's hip. "Loosen up, my dead-hearted friend. Seb needs some cheering up." Then he resumed singing, adding more shimmy to his shake.

"Save it for work," Diego begged but cracked a smile.

With that mantra in mind, I told myself not to glance toward Nova's apartment and not to think of Gianna being over there.

Within seconds, I failed.

LATER THAT AFTERNOON, Nova found me in the living room.

She plopped down beside me. "What's going on with you and Gianna?"

I grinned. "We had a good time."

She bent her head and lowered her voice. "You know what I mean."

The smile fell from my face as I exhaled. "Oh. In that my wolf thought she was my mate?"

"Yes. That's… A problem."

"I know." I ran my hand over my beard. "The sex was great, but I'm not interested in getting involved." My wolf growled at me.

She slanted her gaze. "You aren't?"

"No."

Nova studied me some more. "Gianna is half-siren. Guys often flock to her and act weird."

"It's not like that," I said.

"Then what is it?"

"I can't let my wolf guide me with this foolish desire for a stranger because of how she *smells*," I dismissed. "It's ludicrous. Besides, I'm happy with the way my life is."

"Well, that's good because Gianna is not interested in a relationship."

"Right." I gritted my teeth. "She made that clear."

"She likes her freedom. I don't see her giving it up for anyone."

My wolf grew increasingly distressed by this conversation.

"Then it's settled, isn't it?" I tapped my foot. "We had a good time last night. Today, we're going our own ways."

"I guess so."

My wolf yipped at me with increasing desperation. *She's. Our. Mate.*

I scowled. In a smaller voice, I asked Nova, "What if it's not that easy?"

Nova narrowed her eyes. "What do you mean?"

"What if I can't forget her?"

Her eyes widened. "Oh, Sebastian. You must. Otherwise, you're setting yourself up for rejection."

My wolf moaned. Being rejected by a mate was the worst fate for any shifter.

"Listen, I know this sucks," Nova added in a gentler tone. "Unrequited feelings are brutal. But if you can stop this now, it will keep you from getting hurt."

"Right, right," I declared, seeking a new resolve. "I just needed to scratch that itch." With a clap of my hands, I added, "Done."

Nova stared at me with wariness in her eyes, as if unconvinced. "I hope you're right."

So did I. Any other option would only be disastrous.

CHAPTER 6

GIANNA

At work that evening, after I took care of some reorders from vendors, I checked in with staff and ensured operations were running smoothly. It was a Wednesday, so it was slower than the weekends, but we still had a decent crowd. I sat at the bar and drank my favorite champagne cocktail. What I needed was some fun. Work was done, and mama wanted to play.

Motley Crue's "Girls, Girls, Girls" came on, and I instinctively tapped my feet along with the music. Down at the other end of the bar, a hot guy with dark hair that extended past his chin smiled at me. I returned it, keeping my gaze on his for a tad longer than one of a general greeting, a subtle invitation noting my interest.

Within a minute, he'd walked over and asked how I was doing. Within another minute, I knew his name was Ryan and that he was visiting from the West Coast. He'd be my perfect playmate for the night.

We ordered another drink and chatted about general bullshit until I was ready to go.

"Want to go outside and get some air?" I suggested.

His pretty blue eyes widened. "Sure."

We exited the club, and I steered us around to the side of the building. The January night had a chill, but it was clear. Before I took him home, I wanted to sample the goods. If he slobbered all over me when he kissed or did something else that was a turn off, I'd cut him loose and restart my search for a partner. No point in bringing him to my place or going back to his if it didn't promise to be pleasurable.

"Come here, Ryan," I said. When he stepped closer, I looped my arm around the back of his neck and leaned up to kiss him.

He swooped in with enthusiasm. Our lips touched—and I recoiled.

What the hell was that about?

"Something wrong?" he asked, brows furrowing with confusion.

I assessed the situation to detect a reason for my peculiar reaction. Did he smell bad or have bad breath? No, nothing like that. He was tall, fit, and attractive.

"No, nothing at all." I gave him a sweet smile and leaned in again for the kiss.

Once again, our lips touched. He pulled me into his arms, but I immediately wiggled out of them and away.

Ryan blinked at me. "You're giving me mixed signals here."

No shit, I was doing the same thing to myself. Why? This shouldn't be happening.

Sebastian's face and our hot encounter came to mind. Terrible timing. Why was I thinking of him now? That was a one-night thing. *One* night.

His lips had been so soft and sensual. His beard tickled yet felt good brushing against my cheek. I wanted to look into his deep brown eyes before I kissed him again, feeling that spark ignite between us once more.

I backed away from Ryan. "Sorry, this was a bad idea. I need to go."

Before Ryan could ask any more questions, I rushed back into the club and went to my office. My heart was beating faster as I tried to sort through what had just happened.

What I wanted was vivid in my mind—or *who*, rather.

Ah, hell. I shouldn't call him after that whole mate thing. I'd be sending him mixed signals, too.

On the other hand, Sebastian had assured me that his wolf was just confused.

He wanted to get together again. I wanted to see him again. We were both adults. Was there any reason we shouldn't get together for one more night?

No.

I picked up my phone and texted him. *Are you home?*

No, at work.

When will you be done?

A couple of hours.

Ugh, so long. *Can I come over then?*

Of course.

I exhaled. There was only one person who could scratch my particular itch tonight, and that was a burly wolf shifter.

After another minute, he texted, *Are you okay?*

I smiled. Most guys would jump at the possibility of a booty call, no questions asked.

Yes. Just thinking of you... And what we can do together.

I held back on adding an eggplant emoji and laughed.

Now I'm thinking about it, he texted back.

Oh, the ellipses, it could mean so much. I leaned back in my desk chair and fantasized about the night ahead.

After a few minutes, another text from Sebastian came through. *I can get out of here sooner. Half an hour work for you?*

I rolled my desk chair back, pleased with how a few texts had led me to exactly what I craved.

Perfect. I'll meet you at your place.

SEBASTIAN

What a brilliant surprise to hear from Gianna, especially after she'd stated that what we had would not happen again. After those texts, there was no way I was going to waste time at work. It wasn't a busy night, and the others could handle it.

Once I rushed home and took a quick shower, I barely had time to dry off before she arrived.

I opened the door. She stood in the entryway wearing a black motorcycle jacket, boots, and a Mona Lisa smile. My pulse jolted, while my wolf stirred about. "Gianna, come in." I stepped aside and welcomed her.

"Are you alone?" she asked.

"Yes. Lucas and Diego are both working." I closed the door.

Before I'd taken a step inside, she moved closer. Her vanilla scent wrapped around me, and I inhaled.

Mate, my wolf declared as if I hadn't heard him the previous dozens of times.

Gianna took my collar in both hands. "Good because I want to be alone with you." She leaned closer and kissed me.

The tingling connection I'd only ever felt with her returned. Once her lips were on mine, my arms were around her. Our mouths crashed with greedy hunger as we devoured each other, somehow backing to the sofa and falling onto it.

She pulled my shirt off, trailing her fingers down my chest. "I want to touch you." She then removed her shirt and looked so damn tempting in the black push-up bra.

I moaned, wanting to kiss every bare inch of skin. "Upstairs," I croaked.

She rushed over to the steps, and I chased her up. I grabbed her ass, and whatever I could touch of her along the way, and she giggled. She stripped off the rest of her clothes as soon as we were in my room and then reached for my zipper. "Help me get these off."

I complied and seconds later, stood before her with my erection out. She took it in her hand, and I moaned.

"This is better than any dream," I muttered. "And trust me, this is one of many things I fantasized about you."

She stroked it with a light touch and then gently bit my earlobe. "You tell me. Does this feel real?"

I moaned. "No dream has ever felt this good."

Leading her back onto my bed, I kissed her and skimmed my hands down her body. The scent of her arousal drove me wild with desire, and I couldn't resist tasting her. She moaned and ran her fingers through my hair. Her muscles tightened and her thighs quivered. As she grew closer, my excitement rocketed along with hers.

She shuddered and climaxed, crying out, "Sebastian."

What a phenomenal sound to hear my name in her beautiful voice at the height of rapture. My cock throbbed with a desperate ache to sink inside her.

She was so wet, I slid in without much resistance. She grasped me, wrapping her long legs around my lower back. We rocked together, moans escalating even more with each frantic thrust. She clamped her limbs more tightly and cried out once more.

As she pulsed around my shaft, the exquisite sensation was too much. The pressure grew too powerful. My canines emerged, but I resisted the urge to mark her. I erupted with a feral growl, almost seeing stars in the blackness.

After I came down, I murmured, "I don't know where that came from, but I'm glad about it."

She propped herself on her side and pouted. "I'm not."

"Why?" My heart sank. "Wasn't it good for you?" Hadn't she climaxed twice?

"Oh, it was exceptional," she replied, eyes blazing with accusation.

I blinked at her. "Your expression isn't matching your words, and I'm confused."

She swatted my chest. "You did something to me, didn't you? Put some sort of sex magic or spell on me somehow."

I stared at her, and my mouth fell open. "What? I thought *you* were the siren."

She huffed. "I tried to hook up with a guy at the club tonight. I couldn't."

I placed my hand on my chest as if it could still my rapidly beating heart. "Don't tell me things like that, Gianna." The idea of her with another man pierced me with jealously so sharp, I would have sworn I'd been gutted. "I'm not sure why, but it physically hurts to hear it."

"I didn't want him." Her voice softened. "I wanted you."

Happiness jumbled inside me. "You did?"

"Yes, but that's a problem." She knotted her brows.

"Why?"

"Because..." She raised her hand and flicked her wrist. "Because I'm not interested in a relationship."

I took her hand and kissed the palm. "Why don't we explore exactly what you're interested in?"

"What does that mean?"

Now that I had a chance to have more than the one night she'd promised, I wasn't going to give it up without a fight. "We can be lovers."

She bit her lip as she searched my eyes. After a weighted sigh, she said, "No. I can't commit to anything right now. Not even hot sex."

"Understood." Did I? I stared at the ceiling wondering what just happened. Not that I was complaining about her coming here to seduce me.

I turned to her. "What do you want?"

She sighed and dropped her head back onto the pillow. "I wish I knew."

GIANNA

At work that night, I questioned my earlier decision. Did I really turn down the opportunity for more hot encounters with Sebastian?

Maybe it was for the better. Whatever this weird connection was between us was already confusing enough, and I didn't need any more complications.

An hour later, my mother called me. I was starting to wonder if she would. Knowing her past, I wouldn't be surprised if she had left town already.

"Why don't you come and meet me here in the club?" I told her. It was less personal than my townhouse, my safe space. Although my emotions bubbled and my thoughts jumbled, at least the familiar setting would provide some security.

It was early evening and not at all packed or loud as it had been close to midnight on New Year's Eve. The music played at a lower volume as those who stopped by were often looking for a drink or a bite before they headed home. It was different from the late-night crowd who were eager to drink and have a good time. I asked my bartender, Kylie, to let me know when my mother arrived.

"She looks like me," I explained with a grim expression.

Kylie squinted at my reaction, but I didn't want to get into why I wasn't thrilled about this, so I left it at that and waited in my office.

I texted Nova. *Mommie not-so-dearest is coming by.*

Good luck! she replied. *Keep me posted.*

An hour later, Kylie texted me that my mother arrived. I took a deep breath and gave myself a pep talk before I went to face her.

Stay calm, I reminded myself. *Focus on your questions rather than lashing out accusations.*

Once I stepped into the club, it didn't take long to notice her with her tall stature and dress that was the colors of the ocean. She smiled and walked over to me. Every guy in the bar gaped as they tracked her.

Maybe I should have chosen somewhere with more privacy.

We were here now so we might as well get this uncomfortable conversation started.

I greeted her with a tip of my head but didn't mirror her smile. She didn't deserve it. "Celine." I addressed her by her first name. She also didn't deserve the title of mom.

She turned the smile even brighter as if making up for the lack of mine. Even I was dazzled for a flash, as if she'd entranced me with magic. I wrung my hands as a bout of insecurity churned.

Screw that, I was in my mid-twenties. I'd built up my life without this woman. She would not intimidate me. I raised my chin. "Come, sit down." I led the way to a booth.

Once she sat opposite me, she said, "Gianna, I'm so glad you agreed to meet with me. We have so much to catch up on."

"That's because you haven't been part of my life." I couldn't hold back my resentment. "If you had, we wouldn't be having a conversation like this."

She pouted. "I know this won't be easy for you to understand, but we don't live the way you're used to with humans. We don't need to be constrained by these monogamous bonds."

Then the wolf shifter idea of bonding to a mate forever would also be ridiculous to her. This wasn't time to think about Sebastian, though, so I pushed an image of him out of my mind.

"Where have you been the past twenty-five years?" I asked.

"Moving around. I don't like to stay in the same place for too long."

"Does that mean you haven't been back here since you had me?"

"Right."

"Why would you return now?"

She gave me a sweet smile. "It was time."

That explained nothing. Her answers were more elusive than informational.

I leaned back on the seat and rubbed my forehead. "Are you here alone?"

She shook her head. "I joined up with a pod. We rented a house on the shore to give us access to the sea."

"With other sirens?"

"Mostly."

"And you chose to come to Salem?"

She tilted her head. "Yes, it's right on the sea and is full of magic, which attracts supernatural beings. That's how I ended up visiting here years ago when I met your father."

And then left him with a newborn baby girl. I bit that part back again to keep her talking.

"The wanderlust keeps us traveling. I don't like to stay in one place when there is so much of the world to explore."

She didn't come here specifically to meet me. That hurt. I swallowed the sting. "What do you want with me?"

She flashed the dazzling smile once more, oblivious to my pain. "I'd like to learn more about you. And maybe you'd like to get to know me."

Although a scowl had been pretty much plastered to my face the second I glared at my mother, I couldn't deny my interest. Still, she abandoned me, and she wasn't getting off that easy. "Where have you been since you left me and my father?"

"Oh, all around," she replied with a carefree wave, as if oblivious to my scathing tone. "Mostly the Mediterranean and Caspian Seas. Many sirens live in those areas." She gazed at me and smiled like a proud mother. "Look at you and what you've accomplished at such a young age. I'm so proud of you."

Was she? Although, I would have loved to hear that at any point in my life, it sounded somewhat flat. It didn't fill me with the comfort that I thought it would. There was something about the way she said it that struck me as rehearsed. Like she'd studied things a mother should say. Maybe she had to since she didn't know how to be one. Who was she, really?

I had to focus on my questions. "I've met a few sirens, but they didn't share much." The Salem Supernatural Network connected me to a pod in New Orleans when I was in my late teens. When they'd realized I was only half-siren and couldn't shift to swim like them with fins and tails underwater, they became wary of me. They didn't share much, and their reticence stung. I told myself screw them and returned to live my life with humans.

"I'm not sure what's myth or real," I continued. "And since nobody was around to show me," I bit back more accusatory comments, hoping she'd spill some secrets.

"Don't believe those horror stories about us," she scoffed. "Those tales of sirens luring sailors to their death are pure fabrication, delved up by madmen."

That was another thing that some mean girls in school had given me a hard time about. They'd warn the boys that I'd sing a song that would lead them to their doom.

"If a sailor was lucky enough to spend time with one of us, he'd be having quite an enjoyable time." She arched her brow and gave me a knowing smile.

I squirmed. Thinking of my mother seducing a sailor was *not* what I wanted to picture.

"What about the legends about a siren's song? Is there anything to it?"

I could sing. In fact, I loved to sing, and I thought I had a decent voice. To my knowledge, I had not led anyone to their demise.

"We can express magic though our voices, the same as a witch may use a spell."

I leaned forward. "How?"

She shrugged and then turned her hands palms up. "You put your intention behind your words." Touching her chest, she added, "Energy for any magic starts in here."

With a slow nod, I filed that away for later. Nova and I had to chat about this.

I tipped my head. "What kind of magic?"

She exhaled. "Oh, the usual. Healing. Soothing. Defensive."

I blinked at her. Maybe this type of magic was typical for her, but new to me. "Meaning?"

"You can sing to calm fears, for instance. Or you can sing to confuse an enemy."

Sweet jumping frogs! "I know I'm only half-siren, but is there anything that's different from humans?"

"Well, there's the shapeshifting and the ability to breathe underwater."

I frowned. That was *not* something I was able to do.

"You can do that, right?" she asked, possibly reading the disappointment in my expression.

I leaned back in the booth. "I'm afraid not."

She stared at me. "Huh. That's odd."

"Why?"

"I don't see why you wouldn't be able to."

I squirmed. Nothing like being made to feel inadequate—especially from your mother.

That was likely my perception rather than her intention. I was aware of my issues—many stemming from this stranger leaving me.

"What about, you know—well, sex?" I didn't know how to broach it without saying it straight out. Sirens were said to have healthy libidos. Mine had been roaring as soon as my hormones kicked in, which I attributed to my siren blood. Was there any truth to it?

She brought her fingers together on the tabletop. "That part, fortunately, is true." She grinned. "We're sensual creatures. And sexuality generates its own kind of magic when done right. We're in touch with that side of ourselves, while so many humans are repressed, just going through the motions. That's why we're typically energized by sex." She motioned at me. "Have you discovered that?"

Although I'd never been embarrassed to talk about sex, doing so with my mother did make me squirm. She was my mother, after all—the last person that I wanted to talk to about my sex life— except maybe my father.

"Yes, I've had quite the healthy appetite," I replied. "That's one of the things that Dad and I have clashed about over the years."

My father was so worried I'd end up being like my mother that he tried to keep me home under his watch. As I became a teen, his overbearing ways backfired since I rebelled against his strict rules, sneaking out of the house to see whomever I want. Many arguments with him and my stepmother over my social life led to my decision to move out as soon as I graduated.

"Oh, your father can be so sexually experimental in some ways and then so repressed in others," she scoffed. "When we first got together, he liked to—"

"La la la," I cut her off and plugged my fingers into my ears. "Nobody wants to hear about their parents' sex lives."

She didn't seem the least bit affected by my mortification. "All right."

"What about relationships?" I asked. "Are you with anyone?"

"For the moment." She rolled one shoulder. "I don't like to stick with anyone for too long."

Somehow, I kept from barking out, "Like my father." She was sharing information, and I didn't want to shut it down because of a sullen, defensive attitude.

"A shifter thought I was his mate," I confessed. "Do you think that has anything to do with me being part siren?"

"The poor fool," she replied. "Let's say it wouldn't be the first time a man has fallen for a siren, thinking they'd be together forever."

"Like my father?" I spat. Ah damn, I guess I couldn't hold it in forever.

She exhaled. "Yes, your father thought he was in love with me. He thought that by having a child together, we would stay together. I told him it couldn't be, but he wouldn't listen. He was convinced that once I had you, everything would change. We'd be able to live as a happy family."

"Clearly that didn't happen," I drawled with bitterness.

"I know it's not what you want to hear. Sure, I enjoyed his company and the time we spent together, but it wasn't enough to keep us together. I could never love him the way he wanted."

I ached for my poor, broken-hearted father.

I didn't want to do the same to Sebastian. He was an exceptional lover—giving and insatiable. Some woman would be incredibly lucky to be in a relationship with him. An unfamiliar twist of jealously coiled inside. I would not be that woman. I *could* not be. If anything, I'd end up hurting him.

I couldn't do that to him. It wasn't fair. He was kind, and I could only bring him pain.

"I know you don't understand it," she replied. "That's the human side of you. If you'd been born a full siren, you wouldn't feel bound to stay where you are with those you are with. You'd explore at will. You might decide to leave your pod and join another."

I had the wanderlust bug when I was younger, before I'd established roots. "But I wasn't, and I'm not. Didn't you have any feelings of attachment toward me?"

"Of course, I cared about you."

Although I wanted to believe it, her tone sounded flat—or maybe it was my perception once more.

"Ha," I snorted. "You had a funny way of showing it after not being around—ever."

My mother exhaled, but other than that she didn't show any reaction to my vitriol. No regret, no guilt.

"I'm here now, Gianna. It's time we get to know each other. You can better connect with your siren side." She tightened her lips. "I'm sure you've realized you're not like all these humans." She motioned around the club but didn't break eye contact. "I hope we can get together again while I'm in town," she said.

I arched a brow. "And how long might that be?"

She rubbed her small nose. "If all goes well, we'll be here for some time."

"If what goes well?"

She shrugged. "Oh, you know, adjusting here."

She was evasive in some ways yet provided answers to some of my questions. Did I want to learn more about this world? Would it prove that I didn't belong in either the human or siren one, leaving me somewhere trapped in between?

Belonging nowhere.

She handed me a piece of paper and stood. "Several of us are meeting at the beach house next week. I hope you'll join us?"

"I'll think about it," I replied. No way was I promising this woman anything.

I read what was on the note. It was an address near the shore. "Wait," I called out.

When I glanced up, she was gone. Damn. I had many more questions, but they'd have to wait.

CHAPTER 7

While at work preparing fine cuts of steak at the restaurant, I thought about Gianna. A couple of days had passed, and I still couldn't yank her out of my mind. The desire for her hadn't faded.

Because she's our mate, my wolf insisted.

He had not stopped reminding me of this fact, and how we had to claim her.

How is that even possible? A woman like Gianna did not want to be claimed. She didn't want to have any sort of relationship. That would be an issue. Because now that I had a taste of her, all I wanted was to have more.

After prowling through the house another day, I decided I'd held off enough on contacting her. If I couldn't see her, I at least had to hear her voice.

In my room, I sat on the bed, still detecting a hint of her scent. I called her. After the initial greetings, I asked, "How have you been?"

Gianna groaned. "I met up with my mother yesterday."

"And?" I prodded.

"It was quite a mind bend."

"How about I make you some comfort food? Homemade mac and cheese is always good." My go to was in any difficult situation was offering food. "Actually, anything with cheese is soothing. Whatever you want though, I can whip it up."

Gianna exhaled. "That's a nice offer, Sebastian, but remember what we discussed?"

"What?"

"It sounds like a date, and I'm not interested in dating."

My stomach fell. I forced the words out that no guy wanted to say when it came to a woman he was interested in. "Just as friends."

She arched one of her brows. "Friends, eh?"

"Sure. We have mutual friends, so why not?"

"Does that mean your roommates will be there?" Her wary tone noted her skepticism.

I scowled. That wasn't what I wanted, but if they needed to be there for her to agree, I'd deal with it. "I see them all the time and feed them, but if you feel more comfortable with those knuckleheads around, sure, I'll invite them. And Nova, of course."

"It can't be just Nova and Diego," Gianna said with a laugh. "Otherwise, that seems like a double date."

Would that be so wrong? "I'll invite Lucas, too."

"That sounds—nice. Thanks, Sebastian."

"I'll need to figure out a night when we can all get together. Is there a better one for you?"

"Weeknights are best. The club is busy on the weekend, and I like to be there early to make sure there are no snafus."

"I'll make it happen."

IT TOOK a lot of coaxing my roommates to adjust schedules so I could plan this dinner as soon as possible. We arranged it on a weeknight, which was slower for everyone, and I spent even more time than usual contemplating the possibilities for the menu. Ultimately, I decided for a family-style Italian dinner rather than one too ostentatious, with me showing off my culinary skills as I aimed for a casual, comfortable setting.

When Gianna walked over with Nova and my pulse skyrocketed, I sensed that goal had already imploded. My wolf went wild chanting *mate, mate, mate.*

I gritted my teeth and tried to get him to settle down. Not easy when a dogged wolf was eager to claim his fated mate.

"You look beautiful, Gianna." I walked over and held her upper arms while I kissed her cheek, then the other in the European style.

Her fragrance infused me like a shot of adrenaline. I closed my eyes and let it roll through me. It was as soothing as drinking a hot beverage after coming in from the cold.

"Thanks." Her smile was just as elating.

Nova laughed. "I've never had that kind of greeting from you, Seb."

"Pshaw," I dismissed. "You live here."

"I'll be the one—and only one—to greet you with a proper kiss," Diego said and planted a kiss on her lips.

Lucas groaned and teased, "Get a room." He rubbed the top of Shadow's head, as the cat had slipped into a free spot pressed beside Lucas.

Nova clucked her tongue. "We already have two in this house." She turned to Diego and grinned. "Which one shall we continue in later?"

"Both?" he suggested.

Lucas made a gagging sound. "Couples. Make it stop."

Gianna laughed, a musical sound that warmed my soul. "It smells delicious in here. Did you prepare it all, Sebastian?"

"Of course." I pushed my chest out an inch. "I won't let them in the kitchen with me when I'm working. Can't leave a professional's job to amateurs."

"We get it, you can cook." Diego leaned forward with a mock bow. "All hail Sebastian's culinary magic."

Lucas bowed forward. "We're not worthy," he quoted Wayne's World.

"Fine, you'll go without," I countered with a grin.

"Screw that. It smells too good. I'm not missing this meal." Lucas strode over and took a seat at the table. Shadow jumped off the couch when he stood and darted up the stairs.

After everyone was seated at our table, with Gianna next to me, of course, I introduced the menu for the night and suggested some good wines with which to pair them. "To start, we have artichoke bruschetta. Then a tomato, mozzarella, and basil salad. For the *primi*, we have the classic spaghetti carbonara. For *secondi*, there's chicken pizzaiola. And then for dessert, a tiramisu trifle.

"Ooh, sounds scrumptious," Gianna said.

While we ate, we chatted about life.

"I know this isn't a pleasant topic," Nova said, "but I have to give you all a heads up."

Her tone sounded serious. The muscles in the back of my neck coiled.

"Things have been quiet since the um, incident."

We all knew what she meant. Diego flinched, and Gianna recoiled. They'd both faced that demon and didn't need any reminders.

"Strange occurrences have picked up again," Nova said.

"Like what?" Gianna asked, her face blanched.

"Nothing too terrible. We put out a few fires caused by dark magic. It could just be kids experimenting with magic. But I care about you, and I want you to be vigilant."

"Phew." Gianna exhaled. "Probably just some reckless teens."

"That's what we're hoping," Nova said. "You know the drill. If you see something—"

"Say something," Lucas and I said at the same time.

After that uncomfortable topic was taken care of, we moved on to others. Gianna filled in my roommates on her mother's unexpected arrival.

Then she said, "She invited me to meet her and some others at a beach house they're renting. I haven't yet decided. What would you do in my shoes?"

"Tell her to piss off," Diego declared. "She abandoned you. She doesn't deserve a second chance."

"No," I contested. "This woman owes you answers." I faced Gianna. "You deserve an explanation."

She gave me a thoughtful glance and nodded. "That's what I'm thinking."

Although I was sitting next to her, it wasn't close enough. I resisted the urge to move my chair closer. I ignored the agony of having her so near yet be unable to touch her. At least, she was finally here in my home. I had to take things one excruciating slow step at a time.

GIANNA

Sebastian could cook up a delicious meal, that was for sure. Whoever ended up with him would be pleased in many ways.

Why had I agreed to come here tonight? Once again, my feelings confused me. Could we be friends? Lovers? Was it possible to be both, or a recipe for sure and epic disaster?

After dinner, Diego suggested we move into the living room to play a game.

While we walked in, I whispered to Nova, "A board game? Sounds lame."

"No, it's fun. They've made variations on all of them, pretty much abandoning the rules. When we play Scrabble, we make up words and try to sell them to each other."

I arched a brow. Nova had been caught up in the world of couples and their boring social activity. Since I didn't want to be rude, I'd go along with it.

"What should we play tonight?" Lucas asked rubbing his hands together with excitement.

"Guest's choice," Sebastian replied. "Gianna, do you want to come pick out a game with me?"

Holy tridents. Now it was on me to choose the instrument of boredom? At least I'd be able to pick out the shortest one. No Monopoly.

"Sure." I forced a smile.

Sebastian led me down into the finished basement and opened a cabinet where a stack of board games was stored. I walked by it and over to the instruments set up—two guitars, a bass guitar, drums, a keyboard, a microphone, and amps. Music was far more interesting.

"Are any of these yours?"

"The bass and one guitar. Some just ended up here, so we all dabble with them. Lucas plays guitar, and Diego drums."

"Nice." I shrugged. "That's so cool that you play together."

Sebastian chuckled and ran his hand through his thick hair. "We haven't in a long time."

"Why not?"

"Not sure. Our different schedules, I guess." He arched a brow. "It was hard to find a time for us to even have dinner together."

I motioned at the instruments. "You're all together right now."

Sebastian shook his head. "I can't play in front of you. Not when I'm so rusty."

I tapped his arm. "Oh, come on. I'd love to hear it." Besides, it was better than a *bored* game.

He glanced at me for a few seconds before agreeing. "I'll ask the guys."

Sebastian bounded up the stairs two at a time. A couple of minutes later they all came down.

Diego said, "Gianna, are you crazy? We suck."

Lucas added, "Speak for yourself, dead man walking. We do all right for a basement band."

Sebastian motioned to the microphone and flashed a devilish smile. "You ladies should sing."

Oh, yes. I loved to sing.

Nova spread her hands. "No, way. I can't sing."

"Oh, come on, Nova. You've done karaoke. It would be just like that minus the drunk audience."

"Wait a minute," Diego interrupted. "Gianna, no offense, but do we need a heads up about what happens when you sing?"

"Yes, of course, my voice will lure you into the ocean where you will drown." I kept a straight face for as long as I could as the three guys gaped at me. On seeing Nova's lips twitch in amusement, I burst out with a laugh. "Kidding."

"You got us good." Diego picked up his drumsticks and raised them before sitting behind his set.

"Okay, what should we sing?" Lucas walked over to his bass.

Sebastian picked up one of his guitars and strummed it. "We can't play many songs." He listed some from The Cars, The Killers, The Clash.

"The Killers," I declared. "Mr. Brightside."

Nova and I stepped behind the mic while they started to play. It took plenty of rough starts before they were in synch. After a few more, they played decent enough together for us to join in and sing the lyrics.

We did so, giggling as we screwed up. After several attempts, the five of us were still crappy, but not so crappy for a thrown together basement band.

What fun. I hadn't expected the night to go like this.

When they played Billy Idol's "Hot in the City," Nova and I sang a version we'd started when we were kids. Salem had the nick-name of Witch City, and I'd mistakenly connected the song as "Hot in Witch City," in my mind. It stuck. That was the one time she sang the wrong verse with me. Often, she giggled as I messed up lyrics.

As was what happened in the next song, "When Doves Cry."

I glanced at her, eyebrows raised to ask "what?"

She shook her head and continued to sing, but then a minute later, snickered again. The guys appeared to struggle not to laugh, too, each sporting their own version of a polite smile.

When the song ended, I asked, "What? Did I screw up the lyrics again?"

She laughed. "Some of the things don't make sense. They're not even words."

She was right. She'd teased me about my nonsense lyrics since we were young, and we'd laugh about it. That was the problem with misheard lyrics—they stick in your mind, no matter how ridiculous.

The guys chuckled, too, and I didn't care. They were cool and non-judgmental, and revealing one of my faults made me feel more comfortable around them. She ended up with a good crew, and I was happy for her.

And if I wasn't a screwed-up siren with abandonment issues, maybe I could see myself hanging out more with someone like Sebastian. Someone considerate and fun and a beast in bed.

But that wasn't the case. There was no changing the past, especially with my mother back in town screwing up my present.

SEBASTIAN

Gianna had a beautiful voice, which wasn't surprising. I was already captivated by her and hearing that melodious voice travel through me just added to my fascination. The way she sang the wrong lyrics added to her charms. It made her less perfect and more approachable.

Who would've thought that she would fit so perfectly into my world so soon? Certainly not me. I caught myself staring at her far too often as my yearning grew.

After an hour or so, we ran out of songs we could play at a semi-decent level.

"Who's ready for dessert?" I declared as we returned upstairs. "I made a tiramisu trifle."

"Me," Gianna was the first to say.

I loved her voracious appetite. It was much better than living with a vampire who had little tolerance for food. Whenever I offered him some, he'd scowl like I'd suggested torture on a medieval rack.

"Sign me up," Nova added.

"You know I'm in." Lucas rubbed his flat stomach.

I turned to Diego and cocked my head.

"A little." He pinched this thumb and forefinger together. "Whatever you think a little is, divide it by four."

Ha, typical Diego and his worm-sized belly.

Once I'd scooped out plates for each of us and served it with a sparkling dessert wine, Gianna said, "I never thought I'd say this, but I'm up for a board game if you still want to play."

Hell yes, I was. Anything to keep her here longer. "We have Scrabble, Monopoly, Life, Trivial Pursuit."

"No way to Monopoly." She shook her head. "We could be here all night."

"Scrabble?" Nova suggested.

"The way you play sounds fun. How else do you shake things up?" She bent her head. "Do you have an alternative version of trivia?"

We played it normal, but I was up for switching things up. "Let's come up with one now," I suggested.

After discussing some options, we decided foolishness was best.

"Okay, so question is read as printed," Diego said. "The player responds with a nonsense reply. The reader can counter with a foolish answer."

"How would we decide on whether it works?" Gianna said.

"By laughs," I replied. "If you're the player, and your answer gets a laugh from another player, you go again. If you get more groans, you lose your turn."

It wasn't a solid game plan and was bound to fall apart almost immediately but who cared?

Nova laughed. "It sounds screwed up enough that nobody really wins, but we'll have a good time."

"Works for me." Lucas rubbed his hands together and grinned. "Let the foolishness begin."

He and Diego set up the game. I brought the bottle of dessert wine over. The more we drank, the more ludicrous the responses.

"Where would you find the Sea of Tranquility?" Diego asked Lucas.

He pointed upstairs. "My bed, of course."

We all groaned at that one except for Lucas, who grinned a mile wide.

"What color is absinthe?" Nova asked Gianna.

"The color of regret," she replied in a deadpan voice that got her laughs and another turn.

"What's the body's largest organ?" Gianna asked me.

I arched one brow. "Do you have to ask?"

Diego grunted. Nova moaned and shook her head. Lucas chuckled. Gianna laughed, which was the only reaction that mattered.

From that point on, the answers often had a naughty edge. Gianna often exchanged glances with me. This strange, fun flirtation turned me on, and I hoped I wouldn't sport wood during the game.

Once Diego sort of won the game by ending up in the middle spot, Lucas said, "I'm heading out. I have a date soon."

"A date?" I repeated. "It's almost eleven. Sounds more like a booty call."

"Potato, po-tah-to." Lucas helped put away the game. "Toodles. Don't wait up for me."

Nova put her hand down on Diego's thigh. "I'm ready to go unwind myself. I have an appointment at the Network tomorrow morning and want to make sure I get enough sleep."

A detective from the Network had recognized Nova's magical talent after she'd taken down a demon who'd kidnapped Gianna. I'd heard about the encounter but hadn't met Gianna until the night at the club. Now, just thinking of anyone bringing any distress to Gianna stirred me with rage.

Nova stood, and Diego followed. "I'll come over with you."

Gianna met my gaze. Within a minute or so, it was just the two of us left alone in my apartment. A naughty glimmer sparkled in her eyes.

I was almost quivering with need by this point, and my wolf was nipping at the forefront with his now insistent chant—*claim her.*

Gianna's luscious lips curled into a knowing grin. It was too much of an invitation for me to resist. In the next heartbeat, we lunged for each other, tumbling back onto the couch. All the yearning that I'd been suppressing erupted as I caressed her body and kissed her.

She sighed a decadent moan against my lips. How I wanted to hear those sounds from her night after night.

I'd have to be content with what she gave me so I wouldn't waste this moment. I kissed her face and caressed her breasts. Ready to undress her right here and take her on the couch, a sliver of reason rose through the lust. Diego or Lucas could return at any time.

"Let's go to my room," I suggested.

"Yes," she agreed with a saucy smile and ran for the stairs.

I chased her, desire running rampant, and grabbed her ass. She giggled and headed into my room, turning to me with hunger burning bright in her eyes. I closed the door and reached for her, my greedy hands clutching at her sensuous curves.

Within seconds, we shed our clothes and discarded them to the rug. We tumbled onto my bed, kissing and touching and licking. I rubbed my hands all over her soft skin, craving the touch of my mate that had haunted me with an ever-increasing desperation since we'd met.

Fierce need ignited inside as the fire rose. I explored every inch of her, running my hands and lips down her lush body. Her pleasure was more paramount than my own. When I brought her to a climax that left her quivering and gasping for breath, it heightened my hunger.

I buried myself inside her, slipping into this sweet ecstasy. Rocking with increasing thrusts, the pressure intensified, and with it, the raging instinct to claim my fated mate.

Once again, I ignored that urgency before I exploded with a ferocity that left me spellbound.

As we recovered, my senses slowly returned. One night with Gianna hadn't been enough.

Two had only fueled my appetite for her.

And now, this third time, I knew with a certainty what my wolf had been telling me, and I'd been struggling to ignore. Gianna was my mate, the only one for me, and nothing would ever change that.

If she rejected me, which was almost certain to be the case, I doubted I'd be able to recover.

It would destroy me.

CHAPTER 8

GIANNA

*A*fter another explosive night with Sebastian and a mind-bending quickie this morning, he insisted I stayed for breakfast. When I returned to my townhouse, guilt swarmed around me like aggressive wasps. I shouldn't lead Sebastian on by sleeping with him again. Yet I couldn't deny this attraction. I couldn't stay away.

Would I end up hurting him like my mother did my father?

It was time I faced the inevitable and made the phone call I'd been putting off. I had to tell my father what was going on.

When he answered the phone, I said, "Hey Dad, how are you?"

"Fine. We played golf earlier. I'm gonna grill some steaks soon."

He and Marge, my stepmother, moved down to Florida because she wanted to get away from New England winters. She'd harassed him to go almost as soon as they got married, but he'd insisted I finish out school in Salem where there were others with supernatural blood. Whether that was good for me was iffy. The girls loved to slut shame me but at least I had Nova. If we hadn't had each other to rely on to get through the hell of high school, I don't know what would've happened.

Right, this had been the better option for me. It was better to be an outcast with another freak in my pod than to be alone and on my own.

My father gave me a quick overview of their highlights, which included golf, barbecues, and more blah, blah, blah. We were never close, and we didn't speak that often since I'd moved out. At first, it was about once a week. Now, it was around every month, basically to let him know that I was still alive.

I assured him that I was doing fine before I launched into the bombshell reason of my call. "Someone unexpected showed up at the club on New Year's Eve."

"Who?" He asked in a casual tone as if expecting it to be a former schoolmate or something.

I pursed my lips and then admitted, "My mother."

"Your *what*?" he barked into the phone.

I held the phone a few inches from my ear and stared at it. Sure, I expected surprise, but there was pure vehemence in his voice.

"My mother stopped by the club," I repeated.

After a few palpable seconds passed, he asked, "What did she want?" His voice was edged with contempt.

"She said she was in town and wanted to get to know me."

"I don't believe it," he dismissed. "I don't believe anything that woman says. If she came to you after all this time, it's because she wants something."

Although I'd been wary of her myself, my decades-long clashing with my father put me on the defensive. "You don't know that for certain, Dad."

He snorted. "I know that woman and wouldn't trust her with anything."

I bit my lip as I glanced outside the window and counted to five. The finely manicured grounds of the townhouse rested under a snowy blanket for the winter, including the rhododendron that I loved to see in bloom. "You knew her twenty-five years ago. Who knows how she's changed since then? Maybe she's mellowed with time and regrets leaving."

"No, not her. Whatever she says, don't believe it. In fact, you should avoid her completely."

I knew he would react negatively to hearing this news, but telling me not to see my own mother?

"Dad, I've spent my life wondering who she is and why she left. I want answers."

He was quiet for a few seconds. "I understand that, Gianna." His voice was gentler. "But she's trouble. She is incapable of loving you the way you deserve. That's why she left. She's cold and heartless and will only end up hurting you more. I'm telling you for your own good—you must stay away from her."

I gritted my teeth. He'd often told me things 'for my own good.' "I'm not going to do that. I need to know more about who I am."

"It's a bad idea." The tense warning in his tone indicated we wouldn't find any common ground in this conversation.

I had to end the call before we ended up in a screaming match like the many we'd had when I was a teenager. He'd tried to control me. I resisted. He put more restrictions on my life. I rebelled. And on and on.

"I've got to go," I declared.

"Gianna—"

"Bye, Dad." I ended the call and threw the phone onto the sofa. As I paced through my living room, my breath came hard. I twisted my hair, wrapping it around my fingers and then repeated it.

All the frustrations from our past differences welled up. He'd been overprotective my entire life. Terrified I'd end up gallivanting about like my mother, he kept me as sheltered as possible. He'd tried to keep me safe, but it was suffocating. I'd yearned to be free, roam, explore, and experience life. The more he'd curtailed my freedom, the more I resented him.

When he'd married that bitch, Marge, she'd made things a thousand times worse. She constantly pestered me, telling me how to dress and act. She criticized everything, insinuating I'd be perceived as a whore.

They forbade me from dating, and that sparked my rebellion. I was half-siren and wouldn't be ashamed of it. I'd do whatever I pleased. And why not, since I was accused of much worse?

My father knew nothing about my mother anymore. He could have been just as guilty of slut shaming and slamming her all these years the way I'd been by the mean girls growing up. If there was anyone who could understand being falsely slandered, it was me.

Maybe I'd been looking at my mother from one angle for far too long. I knew what my father was like. He might have driven her away the same way he'd done to me.

Perhaps it was time to give her the benefit of the doubt.

***

WHILE I TRUDGED along the shore the next day, Sebastian called. A few inches of snow had fallen overnight, and the sea breeze wasn't biting, but I still had to pull up my furry hood when it rolled in.

I'd gone for a swim earlier and was still salty about the conversation with my father, unable to keep the foul mood from my voice.

"Is something wrong, Gianna?" he asked.

Did he really want to hear this? Since I'd already told him about the situation with my mother, it didn't hurt to give him a condensed version. "I talked to my father yesterday and told him about my mother being in town."

"I'm guessing he didn't take it well."

"Not at all." I maneuvered around driftwood tangled up in seaweed. "He's not her biggest fan considering she ran out on him and left him with a newborn."

"That must have been tough." He exhaled. "How are you taking it?"

A gust of wind rolled in, and I wrapped my free arm around myself before I could reply. "I'm still coming to terms with everything." I laughed. "Or trying to avoid dealing with it."

"Sounds like you could use some more comfort food."

"Is that your answer to all of life's problems?" I teased.

"Or comfort sex."

I giggled. He suggested it in a playful tone, but it was highly appealing. "Tempting, but I have plans to meet up with Nova for dinner later."

"Where are you going?"

I gazed at the stretch of horizon ahead with the afternoon sun bright over the ocean. "Not sure."

"You could come to my restaurant. I'm working tonight. It would be my treat."

"Sebastian, you don't have to do that. You don't need to take care of me."

"I know I don't. But I like to."

I was used to being independent, insisting I take care of myself, but the way Sebastian offered me food and an ear to listen to my problems was kind of nice. What that meant between us, I wasn't sure. I didn't want to lead him on.

Were we becoming friends?

Ha, I didn't have irresistible urges to sleep with any of my other friends. And I *did* want to see him again.

"Thanks, Sebastian. You're really sweet. I'd love to come down with Nova."

"Great. Just let me know when and I'll handle everything."

"Seven."

"Got it. See you tonight."

"Wait," I stopped him. "I didn't even ask how you're doing."

"Now that I've talked to you, Gianna, everything is absolutely terrific."

We ended the call. I bit my lower lip. Where we stood was confusing, as well as where I wanted us to be.

Why question it? We both enjoyed each other's company. It didn't have to mean anything other than that.

***

LATER THAT EVENING, Nova sat across from me in Sebastian's restaurant. Our round table was covered by a crisp, white tablecloth, daisies in a glass stem-vase, and a tea light candle.

"This is a step up from my club," I noted with a wry grin. Although the food we served tasty, it was pub food served at booths or small tables sans tablecloths.

Nova laughed and spread her napkin on her lap. "It depends on the mood you're going for."

With the waitstaff wearing black and white outfits, shiny black shoes, and a maître d, this restaurant had a classy vibe going on. Soft music played in the background. The air was rich with the scent of delicious meals. Many of the items on the menu were described with flair, noting their local sourcing, and they were rather pricy. Definitely more of a special occasion place rather than a quick bite.

Sebastian came out after we had our wine glasses filled. He wore a white chef uniform, and damn, he filled it out well. "I'll take good care of you tonight."

Heated awareness swept through my body, the way it often did around him.

He pointed to the menu. "You need to try everything." Then he said, "I'll bring you a little of each."

"You don't need to convince me," I said.

Nova agreed.

He brought out the juiciest cuts of steak, and I moaned. We ate coconut-crusted seafood, eggplant bruschetta, stuffed mushrooms, and more.

Minutes later, Sebastian checked on us. "Is everything good?"

"Spectacular," I assured him.

Once Nova and I slowed down on devouring every delicious item Sebastian brought out, our conversation turned to my recent turmoil. I told her about the call with my father. We'd known each other since we were kids, so she knew what he was like—strict, overbearing, and overprotective.

"You and your dad going at it over your mom?" She made a hissing sound and recoiled. "That must have been as calm as a storm in a cauldron."

"Yeah," I released a rueful grunt. "Butting heads since I hit puberty." I took a big swig of wine. "Check you out with your witch metaphors. I like seeing you embrace that side of yourself."

"You know, Gianna, you could do the same with accepting your nature. You're not just a siren or human, but both. And what that means is you don't have to be defined or limited by either. You're Gianna. You can be whoever the hell you want because you're a bad ass who does whatever she sets her mind to do."

I laughed. "Thanks for the moral support."

Sebastian returned. "Need more wine? Ready for dessert?"

"I don't think I can eat another bite." Nova covered her stomach. "Everything was so good."

"Mmm…" I was just as full, but the food was so good. Me and my voracious appetite. "What kind of desserts?"

He listed some. "My favorite is the chocolate tarte with a scoop of vanilla ice cream."

"Ooh, sounds decadent." I reached across the table and touched Nova's hand. "Split it with me."

"Twist my arm," she declared with a grin.

I faked the gesture and beamed at Sebastian. "We'll share one."

My stare followed him as he walked back into the kitchen.

"What's going on with you two?" Nova asked.

Dragging my gaze back to Nova, I said, "We're just friends."

"Who sleep together." She prodded with raised brows.

"Sometimes." I shrugged.

"Can it lead to something more?" she asked.

I made a doubtful sound and followed it with a dismissive wave. "With me?"

"Yeah, why not?"

"I'm not the relationship type."

"Maybe that was before you met the right person."

That was something to think about. Was that why I'd never been interested in a relationship before now?

"Even if that is a remote possibility," I dismissed, "It's the worst possible time. I can't deny I'm having some sort of identity crisis questioning everything since my mother arrived."

Nova sipped her wine. "I know she's created some turmoil, but I like seeing you together."

"You do?" I leaned back in the chair.

She tipped her head. "Yeah. You both seem—happy."

I blinked a couple of times. Was there any truth to that?

"Maybe you should go out on a date with him," Nova suggested.

My fingers rubbed at the napkin on my lap. "I don't want to be in a relationship." I'd repeated that line many times lately, it seemed. This was the first time it rang hollow.

"You don't have to label it as such," Nova encouraged.

Dating added a complication I didn't need in my life right now. Relationships were complex. But when we all spent time together at their house, we had a great time.

We had an even *better* time alone in his room that night.

"How about the four of us go out together?" I suggested. "You, me, Diego, and Sebastian?"

"Ooh, like a double date?" Nova gushed with wide eyes. "That would be so much fun."

I drummed my fingers on my lap. "Didn't you just say *not* to label it?"

"Ah, yeah," she admitted. "Okay, we'll all go out. It's not a date, just fun. Let's do it!"

SEBASTIAN

Although I'd been busy in the hot kitchen preparing dish after dish, I'd checked on Gianna more than necessary. I couldn't stay away from Gianna for long with her under the same roof.

How could I ignore the urge to take care of her? I loved to feed others, so much so that I made it my life's passion. Sharing a meal brought people together. It was one of life's pleasures. Naturally, that would be even more so with my mate.

The more time I spent with Gianna, the more I wanted to see her. My wolf was right—she was the only one, my mate.

One monstrous problem was that Gianna didn't see us the same way. The repercussions could be disastrous. If she rejected me, I was doomed to live as a rejected wolf. Utterly broken. Everything I feared about my life in a pack would come to fruition in the worst imaginable way.

The only way I could avoid going down this destructive path was to convince Gianna to take a chance with me. Each time we spent together gave me a sliver more of hope.

When I emptied a bottle of madeira wine that I used for flavoring sauce, I dashed down to the wine cellar to retrieve another. As I passed the rows of vintage treasures, I slowed down, careful not to barrel into any delicate bottles.

That's how I had to take things with Gianna, nice and slow. I couldn't barrel into her life like a demanding beast. That's how I'd acted the first night, like a predatorial animal, and it ended up with me tossed into the cold. I had to be patient with Gianna. It wouldn't be easy to woo a woman who didn't want to be wooed.

Orders kept me busy in the kitchen, keeping me from fawning. When they slowed, I went to see Gianna and Nova for a few minutes. They'd just finished up dessert, and Nova excused herself to go to the ladies' room. I took her seat across from Gianna.

"The meal was divine." She leaned closer and said, "And the dessert was almost better than sex," in a lower voice.

I laughed. "That's quite a compliment for a chef. But considering our other encounters, it might be an insult."

She reached under the table and squeezed my thigh. "That's why I said almost."

Her touch stirred me with images of what I'd do with her in my bed later. "I'll take it as a compliment then," I replied.

"Good, that was how it was intended." Her smile had a hint of sensuality that drove me wild.

I had to be strategic about this and think it through. If I established our relationship as occasional hookups, it could fizzle out quickly. She'd think of me as a temporary partner and move on.

She took a sip of her wine. "This dessert wine is exquisite."

My gaze locked on the sheen on her lips. "I thought you'd like it."

Despite the desperate longing to be with her, I shouldn't make any moves on her tonight. With our connection, it seemed like we had the potential to build something. Maybe it was just a friendship. If so, that was much more important and longer lasting than a hookup. Wasn't friendship critical for a healthy relationship?

What did I know? I'd never been in a serious relationship. I'd enjoyed my life as a single guy, especially since I'd met up with Lucas. We were happy to go on the hunt together while Diego brooded alone at home.

The sensuality brewing in her now stormy-blue eyes was as potent as a legendary siren song. It took all my willpower not to invite her home with me.

Nova returned to the table, and I stood.

I stole the moment to regroup. "I hope you both had a wonderful night."

Nova thanked me and took her seat. Gianna tipped her head and assessed me with a perplexed expression. Was she surprised I hadn't suggested getting together later? I'd been practically falling all over her since we met.

"Good night." I forced myself to turn and head back toward the kitchen while my feet felt like sludge. My wolf growled in disapproval.

"Sebastian," Gianna called.

The call of her beautiful voice lured me back to her.

"Thank you for a wonderful dinner." She searched me with an earnest expression, which left me speechless.

I gulped. "You're welcome. It was all my pleasure."

When I turned to walk away, she said, "Wait."

"Yes?" I turned back.

"Nova and I were just talking about the four of us going out together—you, me, Nova, and Diego. What do you think?"

My pulse jolted. Was Gianna asking me out? Although it felt like confetti burst inside me, I struggled to remain calm. "Sounds like a great idea."

This time, I turned and strode away with a confident step. I told my wolf, *see—we need to play it for the long haul, not just one night.* Because a woman who did not want a relationship just asked me out on a date.

CHAPTER 9

GIANNA

Color me intrigued by this wolf. I couldn't seem to get Sebastian out of my mind.

Even as I swam the next day, thoughts of him consumed me. Swimming often helped me get out of my head. It wasn't just exercise, but also stress relief. While I tried to focus on my stroke and form, I replayed how sweet and considerate he'd been at the restaurant last night. The surprising part was that he didn't try to sleep with me afterward.

Hmm, I wasn't used to that. Guys were basically walking erections, weren't they?

Maybe we could have something more than casual sex?

Like what? I wasn't interested in a relationship. When I reached the wall, I flipped and swam backstroke down the length of the pool.

Then why did I ask him out with another couple? Ah, this was not the time to add more complications into my life, especially as my anxiety rose about meeting my mother and her pod.

Or was it?

It could be the *best* time. Spending time with Sebastian had been a satisfying distraction. Why not have a little fun and a few more orgasms? As long as we set clear expectations, no one would get hurt, right?

After I finished swimming and showered, I returned to my townhouse to unwind. I had a few hours before heading into the lively atmosphere of the club and enjoyed the quiet of my private oasis.

I made a peanut butter and banana sandwich, one of the meals I often ate during the lean times of saving money for the club. Those were some rough years. I'd worked many side gigs to put more money into the business. Once the club was profitable, I moved on to my next investment with this townhouse and was proud when I signed the papers myself. I didn't have to live off peanut butter sandwiches anymore, but still loved them.

While I ate, I watched a rerun of "What We Do in the Shadows" on the TV. I loved any show with supernaturals. Humans rarely got it right, but when they did, it was fun to guess if it was some writer's imagination or insider knowledge.

After I finished eating, I called Nova to talk about our plan. Funny how much I was looking forward to going out with Sebastian.

"What do you think we should do when we go out on our non-double date," I asked her.

She laughed. "Hmm, what can you do when you have four people," she paused and cleared her throat, "who are most definitely *not* on a date?"

I glanced at some books on my bookshelf, one with adventurous things to do in the area. "We could go into Boston."

"That sounds good. I was looking online for something new to try. Maybe one of those scavenger hunt type of outings."

"That would be better in the spring," I noted. Weather in New England in January could be crappy.

"Yeah, you're right," Nova replied. "We should probably plan for indoors. Like an arcade or escape room."

"Ooh, I thought of something. There's this place where you can do work as a team on solving puzzles. They're shorter, like a few minutes each, so it's not as intense as an hour stuck trying to escape from a room. I went with my staff last year, and we had a great time."

"Perfect. I'll talk to Diego, see when he has the night off."

Before she suggested talking to Sebastian, too, I volunteered. "I'll call Sebastian." It would give me a reason to hear the voice of the shifter who had been in my head far too often today.

After I ended the call with Nova, I called him. "Hey, Sebastian. I just wanted to thank you again for dinner last night."

"It was my pleasure."

His deep, rumbling baritone sent a shiver of heat along my skin. Damn, he had the sexiest voice.

"Anytime you want to stop by or grab some takeout, let me know," he added. "I'll take care of you."

He always did. My breath quickened at the promise in his words, my mind jumping to a sensual scenario instead.

Alas, I was proud to be an independent woman who didn't need a guy, but the way Sebastian looked out for me felt good. Was there anything wrong with that? I couldn't think of any—unless it confined my lifestyle somehow or infringed on my freedom.

"That's sweet of you." I twirled my hair around my fingers. "One day, I'll find a way to treat you just as well." When I heard my flirtatious tone, I straightened and lowered my hand.

"Don't you worry about that, Gianna. I like spending time with you."

As did I, especially with him when we were alone.

"Nova and I were talking about what we could do when we all go out," I said. "We're thinking of going into Boston. Maybe trying one of those puzzle or game rooms. What do you think?"

"Sounds great," he replied.

"Perfect. We just need to figure out a night we can all go." Hopefully soon because I wanted to see Sebastian again—and I didn't want to wait.

* * *

A couple of nights later, Sebastian drove us south toward Boston after sundown. Snowflakes fell but didn't stick and melted as soon as they hit the ground. Whether that would continue throughout the night, we'd see. A few inches of snowfall was expected.

"We need to work as a team," Diego said as we entered the questing area.

We did for the first few challenges, failing two out of three.

"I think I have the hang of it now," Sebastian said as we headed into the fourth one.

It involved a musical pattern. Sebastian tried something that didn't work.

"Don't be ridiculous. That's not right." Diego attempted to step in front of Sebastian to take over.

"Back off, I've got it," Sebastian replied, not letting Diego in.

They pushed each other, each trying to access a knob. Diego used his shoulder to nudge Sebastian away. Sebastian shoved Diego.

"Get out of my way, you furry-assed canine," Diego shouted.

"No, you move, you dead-hearted corpse."

Nova muttered, "Wicked bats and flying monkeys."

I covered my laugh and muttered. "What's next? Are they going to sissy-slap each other?"

She giggled. "That would be entertaining."

I crossed my arms, a smile lingering on my face. "Are they always like this?"

"Pretty much. They're like brothers, rumbling to tear each other apart one minute and hanging out together the next."

We leaned against the wall, amused, as two supernatural men attacked each other over a puzzle that middle schoolers had successfully solved minutes before. Although this wasn't how I thought the evening would go, the amusing distraction was welcome.

Nova groaned. "We'll need to step in if we're going to solve anything today."

"Good plan," I replied.

She wolf-whistled. "Enough, boys. We're running out of time."

That snapped them both out of it. They stared at us, breathing heavy, with hangdog expressions.

Nova motioned to me and then her. "Gianna and I have got this. You figure something else out."

"We do?" I arched my brows at her since I had no clue how to figure out the puzzle.

"No." She laughed. "But we have more of a chance at figuring it out than the two of them beating the crap out of each other."

"True."

Nova and I attempted to solve the puzzle, but time ran out.

"Oh, well." I shrugged.

We left the room.

"We can try again," Sebastian suggested with an enthusiastic gleam in his eye.

I hooked my arm through his and grinned. "I think it's best we let this one go."

He nodded. "You're probably right."

After an hour of fun and sometimes frustrating challenges, we moved on to a dinner and comedy show. This was Sebastian and Diego's suggestion as they were both fans of stand-up comedy.

More snow had fallen, sticking to the trees and giving them a magical look. Without wind, the cool temperature wasn't bad. I stuck my tongue out and caught some snowflakes on my tongue.

Sebastian moaned and leaned close to my ear. "Don't do that," he whispered. "It turns me on."

I stuck my tongue out again and then laughed, flirting again.

Once we entered the club, we ordered food. It was a pub-style menu, so nothing like Sebastian's fine dining from the other night, but still good and hearty. We shared a variety of appetizers, including nachos and buffalo chicken, and pitchers of margaritas and beer.

Several comedians came out over the course of the evening, and we were soon laughing more than eating. Sebastian put his arm behind me as we watched. I leaned against him.

When the show ended, we headed back to the car to return to Salem. I couldn't believe our outing was already coming to an end.

"The whole night went by so fast," I said. "We should do this again."

"Absolutely," Sebastian agreed. Nova and Diego echoed the statement.

Sebastian drove to my house first. That made sense as they lived together, but it meant I had to say goodbye.

Too bad he didn't invite me home with him. Was he taking a gentleman's approach again? It was starting to drive me crazy.

"Sebastian, can you walk me through the door?" I asked.

"Of course."

As we walked from the parking space to my townhouse, I sensed how close he walked. Sensual tension simmered between us. When his fingers brushed mine, I exhaled.

Once we were out of earshot at my front door, I bent forward and kissed his cheek. "Why don't you come back here after you drop them off?"

When I pulled back, Sebastian's eyes gleamed with excitement. "I'll be back as fast as I can."

Once I entered and closed the door behind me, I plopped on the sofa and played music. How much time would I have to kill before he returned? I might as well freshen up while I waited. I headed into the bathroom. I'd just about finished up when the bell rang.

Who would that be? I wasn't expecting anyone but Sebastian, but he wouldn't be back so soon.

I glanced out the peephole. It was him. The excitement that rose was surprising, but I threw the door open.

"How did you get back already?"

He flashed a devilish grin. "I told them to take the car."

I pulled him inside and shut the door. "Smart."

He peered down at me. "One of them can pick me up. Or, if you wouldn't mind giving me a ride home later."

I tipped my head and gave him a suggestive smile. "How about I give you a ride now? And then a ride home tomorrow morning?"

SEBASTIAN

What a brilliant end to an already fantastic night. Not only did I have a great time out with Gianna, but she invited me home with her. This was even after how Diego and I had acted like competitive dumbasses while trying to solve a puzzle earlier.

I'd been careful not to come on too strong during the night, so as not to push my luck, but when I'd put my arm around her in the comedy club, she hadn't pulled away. Where we stood in the space between friends and lovers was still murky.

"Make yourself comfortable." She brushed my upper arm as we headed inside her townhouse. "Let me take your coat."

I removed it and she hung it on her coat hook. She took off her boots, so I removed mine putting them side by side in this entryway. Together. That was the way it would be if my wolf had anything to say about it.

The universe had gifted me with the most wonderful woman as my mate but added a cruel twist with her reluctance to commit. Gianna was a complicated woman who did not want to be chained by a relationship. I understood that desire—hell, I'd been living that way for my adult life—yet it crumbled the more I spent time with her. I wanted to be with her and only her. Could she ever see me the same way?

"Would you like a drink?" she asked.

"Sure. Whatever you're having."

While she continued down into the kitchen, I glanced around the living room and sat on the blue velvet sofa. Soft music played at a low volume, going along with the relaxing vibe. It seemed perfect for someone to decompress after a long night at a rock club. I leaned back, closing my eyes to listen to the song, Morphine's "Cure for Pain."

"You're not falling asleep on me, are you?" Gianna teased as she returned with two drinks.

I opened my eyes and accepted the offered drink.

"Hell no. Just enjoying the comfortable couch."

She sat beside me and sipped her drink. "Right. I enjoy relaxing here to decompress after work."

"I like it," I noted. "I'm glad you invited me here."

"Me, too." She put her drink on a coaster on the coffee table. Then she moved closer to me.

I put my glass down on a coaster beside hers. She tipped her face up and kissed me.

"Let's go upstairs."

I followed her up to her room, excitement enthralling me. My wolf bounded about inside, harping at me to claim Gianna. That was still an enormous, invisible elephant in the room. I hadn't told her the truth. She meant more to me than she knew. This was so much more than just sex for me.

One day soon, I had to summon the courage to confide this to her, despite the crippling anxiety of how she'd react.

Was there the tiniest sliver of hope that she'd embrace our connection?

Or was I doomed to face a devastating rejection?

GIANNA

The day arrived that I'd arranged to meet my mother. Anxiety swirled around me like a low fog. Fortunately, Sebastian distracted me with a steamy quickie in the shower followed by breakfast.

We ate eggs and bacon at my two-seater round kitchen table, which overlooked the small patio. This wasn't a typical scenario I had with any of my lovers. Sex was sex, and I avoided any form of intimacy. But Sebastian wasn't typical of anyone I'd been with in the past.

I sipped the delicious hot coffee while snowflakes fell outside. They didn't appear to stick, though, melting as soon as they landed.

"Are you going to be okay today?" he asked, concern edging his tone.

I adjusted in the hardwood chair. "Yeah. Fortunately, this hearty breakfast will fortify me to face what's ahead." I smiled and then added, "Plus, your exceptional bedroom skills have been stellar at distracting me."

Sebastian's expression fell, surprising since I'd just contemplated his sexual prowess. "What's wrong?"

"Gianna, I need to tell you something." He stared outside the window before bringing his gaze to meet mine. "The thing is— what we have going on means more to me than just sex."

I rolled one shoulder. "Right, we're friends, too. I get that."

"No..." He ran a hand through his thick, dark hair. "What I mean is..."

When he paused, I prodded, "What?"

"I have—" He paused and stared outside again. He brought his hands together, bringing the fingertips to his mouth. "I don't know how to say this."

I shrugged. "Just—say the words." That wasn't exactly helpful encouragement, but his tension started to affect me.

"My feelings for you are… They're more than just friendship."

I pursed my lips as I stared down at my nearly empty plate. "You know how I feel about relationships."

"Right." His tone turned wary.

"Nothing has changed there."

"Oh."

How he could convey so much dejection in that short syllable struck me with a painful twist. I didn't want to hurt him. I didn't want to lose him.

But I still didn't know what the hell I wanted.

"Since I obviously can't stay away from you and your sexual prowess," I teased to lighten the serious vibe, "Maybe we should be lovers."

When I raised my gaze to meet his troubled ones, they gleamed with more hope.

He nodded. "Yes."

"For a little while," I added. "Until we get whatever it is between us out of our systems."

Sebastian cocked his head. "What if that doesn't happen?"

I exhaled and wrapped both hands around my mug. "Sebastian, you know I'm already out of sorts on meeting my mother tonight. Please don't heap anything else onto me right now."

"Understood." He reached across the table and touched one of my hands, still clutching my mug. "Could you consider one thing for me, Gianna?"

"What?"

"Can we keep this exclusive? Don't sleep with another guy. My wolf can't take it." He gulped. "And neither can I."

I hadn't wanted to. And the idea of Sebastian with anyone else stabbed me with a jealous twist. "That means you won't sleep with anyone else, too, right?"

"Right."

"Okay," I agreed. "For now."

IT WAS time to drive to the beach house. Tension crept around me like an irksome shadow, making it nearly impossible for me to sit still. I drove my red coupe to the address, a weathered-shingled, two-story house with snow-covered Rose of Sharon bushes on the shore. I pulled into the driveway and then climbed out, anxiety weighing my steps as I walked to the front door.

After I knocked, my mother answered, wearing a flowing, sea-green dress. "Gianna. I'm so glad you came." She stepped aside. "Come on in and I'll introduce you to the others."

I followed my mother into the house, which went overboard with the beach décor. Seashells and seaside paintings were prominent. Around a dozen people milled about inside, mostly women who were flawless and beautiful. Many held red plastic cups as if this was a college party.

"Everyone, this is my daughter Gianna," my mother announced with a wide smile.

What the hell had I walked into?

CHAPTER 10

GIANNA

My mother introduced me to a trio of gorgeous women. The one with silvery-white hair and pale blue eyes was Aurora, another with amethyst-tinged dark hair and reddish-brown ochre skin was Elle, and the third with tawny hair, bright green eyes, and golden skin as Marietta.

They each greeted me with a cool tone and neutral smile, gazing at me with a wary assessment. Was their unfriendly vibe because I was a stranger they didn't know if they could trust—the same caution as the New Orleans pod? Or more competition for the two men present? Either way, it didn't faze me. I'd faced icier bitches in my life.

My mother then led me to a man who was tall, broad, and blond. "This is Max." She rubbed her hand on his upper arm and gazed at him with adoration. He stared at her, appearing enamored, but he managed to tear his gaze away to greet me with a smile that vanished by the time it reached his eyes.

"Welcome, Gianna. We're glad you came."

"Thanks. What is this anyway? What's going on here?"

"It's just a get together," my mother said.

"Are they all sirens?" I asked her in a low tone.

"No," she replied with a slight smile. "Just the females."

"Come, meet my son," Max said.

Max and my mother continued with introductions before leading me to a man with hair of striking gold like Max. With his high cheekbones and flawless skin, he was almost too beautiful to be real.

"Gianna, this is my son, Jakob."

With how scrumptious he looked, I should have been itching to climb him. My conversation with Sebastian that morning returned. We'd agreed to be exclusive for now. Would it mean I'd be deprived of all sorts of yummy prospects like Jakob? Was that a mistake?

"Hi, there, Gianna," Jakob said in a smooth, velvety tone.

It was nothing like Sebastian's rich baritone that make me all tingly, especially when he spoke dirty.

"Hi."

"We'll let you two chat," my mother said.

That was weird. Why was she setting me up with this guy? Still, he was easy on the eyes and if he had any more answers than my mother, so be it.

She walked away with Max, and they spoke in low murmurs. The other sirens glanced over and whispered among themselves.

"You grew up here?" Jakob asked.

"I did. I just met my mother recently." I cocked my head. "Have you known her long?"

"No. Just in the last two or three months."

I glanced around and noted the food and drinks on display on a table. Neither my mother nor Jakob offered me any. How different from Sebastian. He would have insisted I had a full plate by now.

What did I care? I needed to stop with the comparisons. I didn't need a man to feed me. I could take care of myself.

"I'm guessing your father and my mother are together," I pointed out.

"For now," Jakob said.

Temporary lovers. Was that the way of the siren? It was how I'd lived for many years now, avoiding commitment. It was another reason that I should not be thinking of anything progressing with Sebastian.

"Are you a supe?" I asked him.

"I wouldn't be here if I wasn't," he replied with a sly grin.

Not very informative. He admitted that he wasn't human but hadn't revealed anything else. Maybe he wasn't comfortable around me yet to reveal much about himself. After all, we'd just met, and he didn't know if he could trust me. If my mother and the other sirens were with them, they had to be compatible on some level.

"Meaning you're..." I prompted with a wave of my hand.

"Interested in getting to know you better." He assessed me with a bold, appreciative stare.

My lady parts tingled with awareness, but it quickly vanished. Huh, I would've expected a stronger reaction from myself. After all, he was a stunning male specimen. I should have been picturing a slow seduction right now.

"Ready to go for a swim?" Max asked the group.

My mouth widened in surprise. He had to be joking.

When he and my mom stripped off their clothes right there in the living room, I gaped. The other women were undressing themselves, and I tried not to gape at their gorgeous bodies.

"Come on, let's go," Jakob said.

"Are you crazy?" I asked. "The water will be freezing this time of year." After all, it was January in New England. The only people crazy enough to go in the ocean were those daring enough to run into Boston Harbor on New Year's Day.

He laughed. "You're funny. That won't bother you."

I blinked at him. He didn't indicate anything to reveal he was kidding.

As he removed his clothes, whatever concerns I had faded. Damn, he was something to look at. All bronzed and chiseled. My gaze clung to his V. While he slid his pants down, he revealed he was commando—and well hung.

My mouth watered. It took a lot of willpower to raise my gaze back to meet his.

He had a hint of a smirk on his face. "You're wearing far too many clothes."

My mother called, "Come join us, Gianna." She walked nude out the French doors toward a deck that extended into the harbor.

This is a bad idea, I muttered to myself. Still, curiosity propelled me to go along with it. Jakob strode outside, offering me some sort of privacy as I did so. It was hard to pay attention to what I was doing as my eyes were glued to his stride. His fine ass and strong legs were at a god level.

After I'd removed my clothes, I wrapped my arms over my breasts. Although I typically didn't feel self-conscious, this situation made me far too self-aware.

I followed Jakob out to the beach and tiptoed across the cold sand and onto the dock. Jakob dove off it, resurfacing several dozen feet later where the others bobbed in the water. My mother treaded water near the dock.

"Come on in." As she waved me over, her breasts bounced.

I toed the water off the deck and pulled it back at the icy touch.

"You'll get used to it," she encouraged. "It's easier if you jump in."

Forcing myself to brave the cold, I took a deep breath and then jumped in. Sweet jumping frogs, the water was freakin' cold!

By the time I surfaced, the initial icy bite receded. I treaded water close to her.

"Ready to swim?" she said with a smile.

"I guess."

She took my hand and pulled me with her as she dove under the water. Once I was submerged, I saw the others swimming ahead. Their bodies morphed before me, legs pulling together and forging and then transforming into tails. *Tails.*

Although I'd met the sirens in New Orleans and knew this was possible, I still gaped in awe. Long, vibrant, blue and green tails shimmered as they trailed their beautiful bodies beneath the water. Even Jakob had a silvery-blue tail. What was he—some kind of merman?

I turned to my mother. She'd released my hand as she swam. While she did, her legs transformed from the hips down, fusing together to become a turquoise tail. Astonishment flowed through me as I watched them glide. They each had what looked like gills on the sides of their heads.

My mother swam before me. She did some strange circling motion with her hands and then spread them in my direction. What looked like glowing ribbons swirled through the water and surrounded me. A strange tingling originated in my throat. A flash of terror rose as I feared I had to rush to the surface to be able to gasp air. As I did, it passed just as quickly. Somehow, I knew I could breathe underwater.

What in the wilderness of fucks was going on?

I'd always been able to hold my breath for long periods. The most I'd timed it at was twenty minutes. This was different, it wasn't holding my breath, but actually breathing freely. I reached on the side of my face and color me captivated, but they were there—the strange gills that they had.

A magical tingling traveled from my chest down my core and through my legs. Unable to move them independently any longer, panic clutched my throat. I could still move my lower body, but in a far different way.

Sure enough, a glance at my lower body revealed that my legs were gone and replaced by this long, graceful blue appendage.

I had a tail!

I lumbered with awkwardness until I figured out how to move in this form. How did this happen? After some jerky adjustment, I navigated through the water. The very way I swam changed, becoming much more efficient and streamlined, propelled by this powerful tail.

Mystified, I followed in the direction the others swam, trying to get used to this new experience. Although I'd always been a great swimmer, I'd never sprouted a gill and tails! My mind was blown.

I met up with the pod. All of them moved gracefully as they twirled and swam and moved about beneath the water. I forgot all about the cold and how I should have been freezing. In a strange sort of way, I enjoyed myself.

You're doing great, my mother said. *I knew you would.* She didn't say it through her mouth, but I heard her in my head. I knew beings could communicate telepathically, but I never knew that I was one of them. So many things about what had happened in the last few minutes were ready to blow my freaking mind.

Did you make me shift?

I just helped it along.

A strange calm fell over me. It was as if this was more familiar than I thought. Like I'd done so before.

Maybe it was just the fuzzy edges of a dream. When I was little, I'd often dreamed about what it would be like to swim with my mother. So much longing for the woman who was here now, swimming with me. To make one of your longest and deepest desires come to fruition seemed magical and yet so strange.

After an indeterminate length of time, we swam back to shore. As the water grew shallower, my body seemed to sense the need to change. By the time I was back to be able to stand on the sandy bottom, my tail had split without any sort of pain as my legs returned. I touched the gills on the side of my face. They grew smaller. When I broke through the surface, I gulped for oxygen.

I walked the remaining way, the coolness of the outside air bristling my wet skin, but it wasn't unbearable.

"What did you think?" my mother asked.

My mouth opened and closed before I asked, "Did you know I could do this?"

"Of course," she replied matter-of-factly.

I shook my head, still awed. "I've never shifted before today."

She opened her hand palm up. "Because you never knew it was possible. I just helped you realize your potential."

"How?"

"I used magic to encourage the transformation. You always had it in you."

My mind fog swirled from mild confusion to utter chaos. "Do you generally live underwater?"

"Sometimes more than others. We're of both land and sea and adjust to both."

Some of the sirens ahead found spots beyond the sand to where there was grass. They squeezed the water out of their hair as if sunbathing. Their wet bodies glistened beneath the moonlight.

Jakob caught up with me. "Your first time like that?" He asked.

"Yes," I replied with a slow still somewhat disbelieving nod. "What does this make you—a merman."

"Something like that."

Why was he so cryptic?

He took my hand and led me over to where the sirens were basking in the moonlight. We were all naked, but I didn't feel the least bit self-conscious.

As I found a spot on the grass, I sat alongside them, trying to convince myself that this was all completely normal. My mother was on one side and Jakob on the other.

"Can I shift like that on my own?" I asked.

"Yes," she replied. "Just go in the water and will it to happen."

I furrowed my brows. "It's that easy?"

She nodded. "It's part of who you are, Gianna. You're one of us."

Although those words filled a gap that I'd felt my entire life, not knowing exactly who or what I was, something about this situation struck me as utterly fantastical and insane.

"I want to try it." I stood up and strode back to the water, the grains of sand rubbing between my toes. Once I submerged, I "willed" it to happen. It didn't.

Maybe it wasn't who I was after all. Once again, I was caught in between two worlds and belonged in neither.

I breached the surface and pounded at the water in frustration, spreading a spray of saltwater. I took three deep, calming breaths to focus. For some reason, Sebastian's face appeared in my mind, his gentle eyes encouraging me. I swam beneath the surface, centering my energy.

I focused on shifting to that form again, like thinking of moving a limb. Without thinking too hard, it came naturally.

Magic flowed through me, an odd sealing of my legs binding together before reshaping back into a long tail. The gills emerged, enabling me to breathe underwater again.

Was this how I was truly meant to live?

And was this who I was meant to be?

CHAPTER 11

GIANNA

The next morning, my eyes popped open. I pulled up the covers and exhaled. Oh good, my legs were there.

I touched the sides of my face. Nothing odd.

Had I dreamed what had happened last night? After I crawled out of bed, I wandered into my kitchen still in awe. I ran through my morning routine with making coffee and went over every incredible moment of the night. It had been real.

I wanted to talk to Nova about it, but not go over to her place. The temptation to see Sebastian would be too strong, and I needed girl talk right now, not a booty call.

But maybe later…

I shook my head and texted Nova. *Can you come over?*

Sure, in about an hour or so. Finishing up some work.

To burn through some of the restlessness, I played a salsa dance workout on the TV and followed it in my living room. Then I took a shower being particularly careful about washing my legs. Would they automatically shift when I was in water? That would make swimming at my gym problematic.

I turned on the bath and submerged myself. I tried to initiate the shift the way I had last night. Nothing. Phew. An accidental thought about swimming in siren form while at the gym could have been disastrous otherwise.

When Nova came over later, I told her what had happened at the beach house, hearing the wonder edging my voice.

"Wow, that's crazy!" Her eyes were wide with incredulity.

"I know, right?"

She brought her fingertips to her mouth and then lowered them. "How did you end things with your mother?"

"She asked me to come back and invited me to stay longer."

"Are you going to?"

"I don't know. I'm overwhelmed by everything. I just needed someone to talk to about it."

"You know I'm always here."

"Thanks." Strangely enough, I pictured Sebastian again and his warm eyes. How whenever I was feeling overwhelmed, thinking about him had a way of making me calm.

It was always better when a few orgasms were involved.

"What are you thinking about?" Nova asked.

Aware of the smile that had spread across my face, I wiped it off. "Nothing," I dismissed.

"Uh huh," she replied in a *you're-full-of-crap tone*. "You sure it has nothing to do with Sebastian?"

"Why would you think that?" I asked in surprise.

"You have a dreamy smile on your face. I figured it was a good guess."

Eek, busted. "We're just friends." My tone rose a notch, which didn't help me with selling it—especially since we'd agreed to be lovers, exclusively, for the time being. Besides, who was I trying to sell the friends story to, anyway? Nova or myself?

The lines were blurred. That's why I should have been careful about messing around with Sebastian. Being friends would have been fine. Hooking up a couple of times would have been fun. Mixing up the two and becoming lovers? That's when things started to get complicated. Considering I'd just discovered a surprising new side of myself, it was probably the worst time to add anything new.

All these jumbled emotions churning inside weren't ones I could keep to myself, especially as Nova stared at me. "Okay, Sebastian and I agreed to be exclusive lovers for a short time," I confessed.

"Ah." She nodded. "You're growing feelings for each other."

"Yes. No." I twisted my hair. "I don't know. This is the worst time for it to happen."

"Why?"

"Because my life is so chaotic with everything lately."

"Maybe it's the best time then."

I widened my eyes at her. "Come again?"

"You seem calmer around him. Happy. So, isn't he a positive presence in your life?"

"Yes, maybe, but…" I released my hair, and it fell over one shoulder. "What if I'm not cut out for this? Maybe I'm better suited for casual encounters—with someone like Jakob."

"I guess you'll discover that as you go," Nova replied.

"What if I hurt Sebastian, Nova? I don't want to do that. He's too good for that." Too good for me.

"Give yourself more credit than that. You paint yourself as fickle and unsuited for a relationship, but I know that's not true. Look at you and me. You're the longest, most loyal, closest friend I've ever had."

Hmm, I'd never considered it that way.

Yet there was another possibility that I left unspoken—what if the opposite happened and Sebastian hurt me?

Trusting him left me vulnerable. He could walk away at any time. He could find someone else who wasn't a pain in the ass like me with all my issues.

And then once again, I'd be abandoned.

"HEY LADIES," I greeted Nova and Zoe, the petite, no-nonsense elf who was training Nova to help at the network.

Nova mentioned they'd stop by. "Love the dress," she said.

I twirled, showing more of the black dress with dancing skeletons along the skirt, going along to the beat of the Van Halen song playing. "You should borrow it. You'd look cute in it."

Nova snorted. "I couldn't pull it off like you. I'd look like a goth doll."

Zoe chuckled. She was even shorter than Nova, yet her presence made her seem much taller. "Good to see you again, Gianna."

It had been a while since we'd met on that unfortunate night with Andre. She didn't refer to that time to which I was grateful. Being kidnapped by a demon was among my least favorite of memories.

After we ordered cocktails and sat at a booth, I asked, "How are hijinks in the magical world?"

Zoe frowned. "Our brief reprieve from dark magic seems to be over."

"Oh?" My muscles tightened.

"We had an attempt to infiltrate the Network," Zoe explained.

"Yikes," I replied.

"We're hoping it's nothing to worry about," Nova added. "But be wary."

"Will do." I tipped my head. "Do you have any leads?"

"Nothing significant," Zoe replied. "Keep an eye out for anyone or anything that seems out of place."

After she climbed out of the booth to head to the ladies' room, I glanced at Nova. "Mommie dear, for instance."

"I know, I was thinking about that." Nova tapped her chin.

I stared at her. "I was kidding, Nova. My mother is a siren, like me. Despite the bad rep, we're not evil."

Nova shook her head. "Right, right. Sorry. She's your mother."

Nova even thinking it bothered me. "You're a witch. You know these stories aren't true. Just dudes talking shit about women for some nefarious purpose."

Having grown up in Salem, we were well acquainted with what happened during the witch trials.

"I know. I'm just worried about you, Gianna."

"Why?"

"Something about your mother's arrival doesn't sit right."

I took a sip of my peach cocktail. "Right. She's a shitty mom, but that doesn't mean you need to suspect her of something unrelated."

"You're right." Nova bit her lip. "I just don't want her to hurt you."

I raised my chin. "Don't worry, I can take care of myself." That had been what I'd been telling myself for years. Something came to mind about the last time dark magic had been detected in Salem and witches had been killed. "What about you?" I asked, concern rising. "We should be more concerned with you being a witch if it's anything like last time."

"It's a different pattern," Nova explained. "So don't worry too much. I just want you to be vigilant of anyone now." Her expression appeared tight with worry. "Even of her."

I exhaled with a huff. "You have no reason to suspect my mother of any wrongdoing."

"I know, but maybe we should tell Zoe…"

"Absolutely not," I cut her off. "You can't suspect her just because she's in town. So are thousands of others. Just because she sucks at being maternal doesn't make her evil. You have no reason to connect her with what's going on."

"Okay," Nova agreed with a sheepish look.

Still riled, I added, "This is my mother we're talking about, not some demon. If the Network interrogates her, they might scare her off. I've waited my entire life to meet my mother. Don't screw this up for me, Nova. Okay?"

"Okay."

"Promise?"

"I promise," she agreed. "You're right, and I'm sorry."

Although my heart still pumped faster in my defensive state, I knew Nova was just looking out for me. "It's okay. We're good."

SEBASTIAN

Without trying to smother Gianna, I had to see how she was doing. I'd texted her the day after she'd met her mom to see if she was okay, and she'd said she was fine. It took all my self-control not to try to meet up with her again. How much longer did I have to wait? It was difficult to give her space. Considering all the progress we'd made, I couldn't ruin it by pushing too hard.

I waited until the next day to text again. She noted she'd be at the club all week. I scowled. Was she blowing me off?

What's your next night off? She texted.

Thursday.

Want to come down to the club?

A lightness spread inside my chest. Gianna invited me—just me —to hang out with her. No insistence that Nova or my roommates join us.

Waiting that long to see Gianna again was another herculean effort. I entered the now familiar club with the red and purple lights shining on the dark space with bats on one wall. The sound of Prince's "The Beautiful Ones" surrounded me. The moment I spotted Gianna, wearing a black and purple rockabilly dress near the bar, my breath hitched. My wolf rose with awareness, murmuring *mate*.

Was this how it would always feel when I saw her?

When we made eye contact, my palms heated. I strode over to her forcing a slower, confident swagger to offset my rapid heartbeat. Once I reached her, I hesitated. Would she freak out if I kissed her in public? We hadn't discussed that. Instead, I teased, "I hope I don't get booted on my ass this time."

She countered with a sassy grin. "If you don't act like an ass, I'm sure you can avoid landing on it."

"Fair enough." I laughed and then kissed her on the cheek. That was a friendly greeting, conveying nothing about our intimacy, and her smile lingered. "How did things go with your mother?"

Her lips turned downward. "I don't want to talk about that right now." She perked up. "What can I get you to drink?"

Judging by her expression, whatever happened bothered her. Not wanting to poke at that wound, I wouldn't push her to tell me anything.

I glanced at the drink list. "How about a Gorky Park?" I had their version of Moscow Mules the first night I was here and liked it.

After we each had drinks, she led me to a booth at the back where the music wasn't as loud. She handed me a menu. "Are you hungry? We don't have the fine dining options like you're used to, but I assure you, it's all edible." She quirked a brow.

I laughed. "I'm sure everything is delicious." After sipping my drink, I confirmed it. "Yes, perfect." I motioned around the club. "Did you create all this yourself?"

She nodded. "I made all the major decisions and financed the costs, but others helped with the actual set up."

"I like the vibe." Groups of people congregated around the space, mostly near the bar. There weren't as many as on New Year's Eve, as to be expected, but it appeared to be quite full, boding well for the future of the club. "No wonder it's so successful."

She gave a modest shrug. "Who doesn't like good music?"

"Exactly," I agreed. "This is a great album."

She smiled. "Nova and I listened to *Purple Rain* countless times when we were young."

"You grew up here with her in Salem, right?"

"Yes," she agreed. "We met in elementary school and were friends all through high school."

"Have you always lived in the area?"

She shook her head. "After I graduated, I moved around for a few years—New York, New Orleans, Los Angeles, and more. I worked in clubs and picked up ideas. Also, I worked my ass off to save some money. When I felt it was time to return, I searched for where I could build my dream club. This building had been abandoned and was in rough shape, so I nabbed it at a great price. It took a *lot* longer to get it into a usable condition." She motioned around her. "And now, here we are."

"I'm impressed." I raised my chin. "You should be proud of what you've accomplished."

"I'm happy I can support myself by doing something I love." She took a sip of her drink.

"I can understand that. My primary goal when I left my pack was to take care of myself. Discovering a passion for cooking made it far more enjoyable."

"It shows in what you create. Everything I've tasted has been incredible."

Pride swelled my chest, my mate's admiration warming me.

Gianna tilted her head. "Why did you leave your pack?"

Bitter memories swirling like dark fog in my brain. "I hated living with them. The Sacco pack is awful."

She gazed at me for a few seconds before asking, "How so?"

Why had I revealed my past? I hated even thinking about it. But I didn't want to keep things from Gianna. "We lived in the White Mountains in simple cabins. They dismissed many modern conveniences, choosing to cling to a life I consider backwards. They avoided most others in the region. I wanted to see what else was out there in the world."

"When did you leave?"

"Fifteen. Almost as soon as I was old enough."

"Ah, I left when I graduated high school at eighteen."

I smiled at her. "We have some things in common. Both leaving home as soon as we could to create life on our own terms."

"Exactly. And I'm never turning back." She studied me. "You left at such a young age, though. Was it that bad?"

My muscles tightened, especially the ones in my shoulders. I forced myself to relax them on an exhale. "Since I was a late bloomer, I was picked on being small and scrawny. The older teens said I was worthless to the pack. They harassed me whenever they had the chance."

"That's awful, Sebastian."

A sour taste coated my tongue as I remembered the worst of it. "When I was young, I fell through a frozen pond and almost drowned. It made me incredibly wary of water. They knew my fear and exploited it. They'd drag me into the water and hold me under, laughing as I frantically tried to surface." My ribs seemed to clench around my lungs as that sensation of being unable to breathe return.

Gianna gasped. "They bullied you and made your fears even worse?"

I forced a smile, which likely came out more of a scowl. "I hate water to this day."

She placed her hand on her chest. "Oh, it kills me that they did this to you. Water can be so soothing. I never feel as calm and refreshed as when I'm swimming."

I shook my head with vigor. "Definitely not the case for me. It's more of a desperation to get out."

Gianna reached across the table and touched my hand. "I hate what they did to you. You know there are different types of therapy like that to help you to face and conquer your fear."

"I'm not interested. I'd rather just stay away from the water."

"But what if you need to swim?" She tapped her fingers on the table. "Say something happened, like I don't know—you fell into a pool or off a boat. Would you be able to swim to safety?"

I stared at the black tabletop. "Probably not." The worst scenario played in my mind—being trapped underwater, unable to breathe.

"Humor me, Sebastian. Would you come to the pool with me? I generally go swimming three times a week. I'd love to help you break through this fear."

I gripped the edge of my seat. My limbs felt tight and heavy. I grimaced. "I'd hate for you to see me like that." The last thing I wanted to do was look like a fool in front of her.

"Like what?"

"Afraid."

"No, brave," she declared. "You'd be facing your fear. Everyone has them. Not everyone is courageous enough to take them on."

I searched her eyes, more violet today than blue. "What are you afraid of, Gianna?"

She turned away and took a sip of her drink while glancing around the club. Then she put her drink down. "Being controlled."

That wasn't what I was expecting. I grinned at her. "I thought you might say one of the common fears, like snakes or spiders or heights."

"No, those don't bother me at all." She ran her hands down the stem of her champagne glass. "My father was super strict and overbearing. We clashed often. He was so concerned that I'd end up like my mother and maybe live some kind of wanton life-style." She snorted. "I sure lived up to his expectations, didn't I?"

Since that appeared to be a rhetorical question, I didn't respond.

Her expression darkened. "I hate anyone else controlling me in any way, physically or emotionally." She exhaled with a shudder. "That time with the demon made it worse." She glanced away and rubbed her upper arm.

I only knew the basic details in that a monster had kidnapped Gianna. Fury simmered within me with a yearning for vengeance. But Nova believed she'd banished the demon, so that opportunity was gone.

An urge to care for and protect Gianna grew.

"If there's anything I can ever do for you, Gianna, just ask."

She gave me a warm smile. "Thanks." She then clapped her hands on her thighs. "I want to hear the rest of your story. What did you do after you left your pack?"

I took another gulp of my drink before I continued. "I found odd jobs as I moved over to Maine, mostly in restaurants. That's how I learned to cook. After several years, I'd worked my way down the coast until I ended up in Salem. I heard about the Network, and they helped me get settled and into a culinary school. They later connected me to Diego and Lucas, who are my new family now. My new pack."

"That's wonderful," she said. "I'm glad you all found each other."

"Family doesn't have to be who we are born with," I told her. "You can choose to make your own pack."

She exhaled. "When your family leaves you, you have no choice."

Compassion filled me. "Meaning your mother?"

"Right." She twisted her hair and then tossed it over one shoulder. "The difference is you left. In my case, I was the one left behind. That leaves a hole so deep, I don't know if it can ever be filled."

The yearning to care for and protect her grew ever stronger. What could I do to take away her pain?

"I'm sorry, Gianna, and I hope it's not true. You deserve to be loved and appreciated."

A delighted smile crept at the corners of her mouth. She caught my gaze, and our eyes locked.

"Sebastian, I want you to consider something."

"Like what?"

"Come to the pool with me."

"What?" I stared at her. "No way."

"I'll make it worth your while." Her tone edged higher, and her smile turned flirtatious.

Taken off guard by the sudden shift in tone, I gaped.

"Come with me," she crooned.

"Can't do it." I shook my head. "Although the promise of seeing you in a swimsuit is tempting."

"How about without one?" She arched her brow.

Excitement and fear clashed within. "Even more tempting, you siren," I teased. "Why do you want to do this?"

"You've been kind to me. I'd like to do something for you." She slanted her gaze. "Besides, isn't that what friends do?"

I searched for the answer. "Is that we are—friends? And lovers?"

She bit her lower lip. "It seems like that to me."

I smiled. "I agree." What that meant in our already complicated situation with her being my mate, remained a mystery. "I've never had amazing sex with a friend before."

She laughed. "We will not call this a 'friends-with-benefits' situation."

I covered my heart. "Please don't tell me those benefits are slashed."

She slanted her head. "Depends."

"What?"

"On whether you take up my offer to come to the pool with me."

My pulse quickened. "You minx," I teased. "If that's what I have to face to be with you, I'll suck up my humiliation and expose myself as a fool." As I pictured what I'd just agreed to, fear churned inside, leaving my palms clammy. "Promise me one thing, Gianna."

"What?"

"Don't let me drown."

CHAPTER 12

GIANNA

As I walked toward the gym entrance with Sebastian the next day, he stopped in the parking lot.

When I glanced at him, he was ghostly pale. "Are you okay?"

"Just give me a second." The smile he flashed appeared forced. "I can't believe you convinced me to do this."

Why I had was odd. His fear of water shouldn't matter to me, yet it did. His story had tugged at my heartstrings. Tormented by his pack, no wonder he'd left. He started over without family or friends to make it on his own. I admired and respected that.

Besides, it gave me something else to think about other than my own confused state and my mommy issues.

"Just think." I took his hand and squeezed it. "Much of the fear is in your head. Once you face it, then it will no longer be able to control you."

"You're right." He nodded and resumed walking. "Rationally, I know it's true. But you know what they say about irrational fears?"

"They're irrational?" I replied with a laugh.

"Exactly." He grinned, and a twinge of heat churned in my stomach.

What was it about this shifter that affected me so?

He opened the door and held it for me. Once we checked him in as a guest, I told him, "I'll meet you at the pool."

We went into the separate locker rooms, and I waited for him. After a few minutes passed, I wondered if he was coming. It shouldn't take him much longer than me to change and rinse off.

Over the next couple of minutes, more doubts rose. Did he bail on me?

When the door from the men's locker room opened, and Sebastian walked out, I stared. He looked sinfully alluring in a pair of black swim trunks. Water glistened on his muscular torso. I bit my lower lip as my gaze followed droplets of water rolling down. A woman swimming laps paused at the wall and glanced at him with a longer perusal than was necessary—for my comfort, at least. It twisted me with unease.

Jealousy wasn't an emotion I was well acquainted with, yet this wasn't the first time it had happened since I'd met Sebastian

When his gaze locked on mine, any negativity flitted away.

He strode over. "Sorry, it took a pep talk in the shower to work up the nerve."

"I'm glad you did."

His gaze roamed down my body, clad only in a black swimsuit. "Me, too." When his eyes met mine again, he said, "Mission accomplished.'

"With what?"

He flashed a lopsided grin. "You succeeded in distracting me from what I'm about to do."

I laughed. "We're off to a good start." I cocked my head. "And I'm glad because you've been good at doing the same for me whenever I need it most."

Three people were swimming laps, but the end lane was empty. Although my mother had assured me that I wouldn't now sprout a tail once I entered water, a part of me remained wary.

Fortunately, Sebastian was a shifter, so he wouldn't freak out like a typical human, yet there were a few here. And likely video cameras.

Perhaps, I should have warned him in advance, just in case.

No, I was worrying about nothing. I'd taken a bath, and nothing had happened. I doubted that a much larger version full of chlorine would be different.

We walked down to the shallow end. I took a deep breath and shook off any remaining hesitation.

Then I climbed down the ladder. The pool was heated, which was much more welcoming than the cool ocean. Once my feet were on the bottom, I turned to face Sebastian.

He backed away, eyes wide with terror. "Never mind. I don't think I can do this."

"You can," I encouraged. "Don't think of anything except following me."

"I'd follow you into a volcano, Gianna." He gulped, his face a mask of squeamishness. "But… this is much worse."

I offered my hand. "Don't think about anything but taking my hand."

After a few seconds with his eyes closed and lips moving as if more of that internal pep talk, he popped them back open and fixed his gaze on my face. He bent down and squeezed my hand like he wouldn't let go, his face contorting with turmoil.

"Now just come stand beside me. The water is warm. It will barely reach your waist. You will be absolutely fine," I reassured him. "You can hold my hand the entire time."

He clutched the ladder as he climbed down. As he descended into the pool, his body trembled. He froze and climbed back out.

"Sebastian, don't leave." I touched his calf. "You're doing great. Just take my hand."

He froze on the ladder. "I'm afraid."

I felt for him. I convinced him to come here, and he was terrified. Maybe this was a stupid, selfish idea. We'd gotten this far, though, so I opted for one more push.

"There's nothing to be afraid of, Sebastian. I'm here I won't let anything happen to you. Just come to me."

I rubbed his leg, trying to soothe his fears. "Come to me," I crooned, putting my intention behind the words the way my mother had explained.

"You're doing something, aren't you?" He asked.

"Just assuring you that there's nothing to fear."

He breathed hard. "Whatever you're doing is helping." After several more seconds, he said, "Okay, I'll try once more."

Sebastian descended a step. I kept my hand on him.

"That's it," I encouraged. "Just one step at a time."

He continued to descend and then moved away from the ladder.

He glanced around. "Ahh!" It came out as a high-pitch shriek.

He flapped his arms around, splashing the water like a duck on crack.

I touched his shoulder. "It's okay, Sebastian. You can stand."

He floundered around, expression terrified until his feet met the ground and he stood upright. "Oh." He glanced around, face reddening. "I feel like an idiot. You must think I'm a fool."

I looked around the pool. All the swimmers were in the midst of a lap. Whatever sounds he'd made must've been masked by the water.

"Not at all. I think you're incredibly brave. Don't worry about anyone else. Just keep your eyes on me."

I held his hand. He grasped it as if it was a lifeboat and he was drowning although he was standing on the pool bottom.

He sucked in a sharp breath and shuddered. Since he was a wolf shifter, and they tended to run hot, I ventured it had nothing to do with the cold.

"You did it, Sebastian," I declared, beaming at him. "You took the hardest step." I bent forward and kissed him on the lips.

Sparkles of excitement replaced the terror in his eyes. His lips twitched into a semi-smile.

"Now what do we do?" he asked, his hand still clasping mine in a tight grip.

"You don't have to do anything other than get comfortable in the water."

I bobbed up and down a few inches, submerging more of my body.

His gaze lowered to my breasts and moaned. "Gianna, you are a master of distraction."

I laughed. "That wasn't my intention. But keep your eyes on the girls if that's what it takes."

"You could sign me up for a whole season of lessons if this is the way it would go." He slowly raised his gaze to meet mine and moved up and down barely an inch.

"Perfect," I praised. "That's all you've got to do. Just get comfortable."

Sebastian raised and lowered himself a few more inches up, getting his torso wet, but making odd squelches.

"I'm so proud of you, Sebastian," I said.

We continued to bob up and down in the water, holding hands.

"Doesn't this feel good?" I asked.

"It's not *unbearable*." Then he quirked a smile. "It's even sweeter knowing there's a reward at the end."

For us both. I agreed, "Absolutely."

SEBASTIAN ENDED up spending the night at my place. The next morning, he cooked banana walnut pancakes and sausage while I brewed up the coffee.

While we carried our plates and mugs to the kitchen table, he said, "I still can't believe you got me into the pool yesterday."

"Was it worth it?"

"If you mean by coming back here with you, then hell yeah." He raised his chin and grinned. "It will take me some time to work up the nerve to go back, but with a reward like that, it may be sooner than later."

I laughed and sat down. "With the way you took care of me, I think I was the one rewarded."

"Oh, Gianna, satisfying you is one of my greatest pleasures."

I took a bite of the pancakes and moaned. "You do in so many ways." After I swallowed, I said, "How did I luck out with a guy who's as talented in the kitchen as he is in bed?"

A proud smile flickered on his face. I wondered why I'd said that. Technically, I didn't *have* him. We were just screwing around for a short time. And then when we were ready to move on, hopefully we could remain friends—because I didn't want to lose him as a friend.

I sighed. And I didn't think I wanted to lose him as a lover, either.

"You never told me about what happened with your mother," he said. How did it go?"

My muscles tightened. What I'd discovered was so incredible, I still didn't know how to shape them into words.

I sipped coffee as I debated how to answer. "It was—um—mind-blowing."

"How?"

I exhaled. "It's kind of crazy. Maybe you won't think so since you're a shifter, but she shifted to siren form—fins, tail, and all." I placed my hand on my chest and added. "She did something that helped *me* shift, too."

He knitted his brows together. "Have you never done so before?"

"I would say it's for the first time, but…" I pursed my lips and gazed off out the window. "What's been bugging me is I have the oddest feeling that it wasn't. But that's something I should definitely remember. Doesn't that seem weird?"

"Is it possible you did, and you don't remember?"

"Maybe. I met sirens when I was in New Orleans. When I told them I couldn't shift, they didn't want anything to do with me. The thing is I didn't think I could. I still can't believe it."

When I paused to take another sip, my hands were shaking.

"Are you okay, Gianna?" he asked.

I put the mug down and held onto it with both hands. "Yes, I think so."

"That must have been incredible for you. I've been able to shift my entire life, so I can't imagine how strange it must be to experience it initially. Did you enjoy it?"

I ate another bite of the heavenly pancakes as I considered it. "It felt weird. My body doing something I wasn't accustomed to. But once I grew more comfortable in my new body, it was incredible to be able to swim that way. And there was the bizarre experience of doing all this with my mother, considering our lack of a relationship."

"How did that go?" he asked with concerned eyes.

I pursed my lips. "That, too, is still odd. In some ways, uncomfortable. I mean, despite our biological connection, she's a stranger."

"Right." He nodded. "How did you leave things?"

"She invited me to come back and spend more time with her at the beach house she's renting—her and the other sirens she's traveling with."

"Do you think you will?"

"I don't know. I'm still adjusting to everything."

He nodded. "You don't owe her anything. You do whatever is best for you, Gianna."

I reached across the table and touched his arm. "Thanks for looking out for me."

After we finished breakfast, Sebastian left, saying he'd get out of my hair. Although the old me would have been happy to push him away, it would have been nice to hang out with him longer before we each had to go to work.

Ugh, that sounded more like a relationship thing to say. What was happening to me?

After confiding what had happened with my mother to Sebastian, it was easier to sort through the chaos in my head.

NOVA MET me at the club for a drink the next night.

"Something's been bothering me about what you said about shifting for the first time." Her brows were tight with worry.

"What?"

"It's odd that you weren't able to shift until she did something."

I shrugged. "I didn't know I was capable of it to even know it was an option."

"No, that's not what I mean." She meshed her lips together. "You know that my parents had my aunt block my magic when I was young. So, I'm wondering—did something like that happen with you?"

My pulse quickened, but I brushed my unease off with a wave. "No, that can't be right, Nova. I'm only half-siren. I grew up around humans. I didn't know it was even possible."

While we continued to chat, what Nova said pinged at the back of my mind like a determined mosquito. It continued through the night, disrupting my sleep.

The next morning, I brewed a strong batch of coffee before making a call that might put this question to rest.

CHAPTER 13

GIANNA

"*H*i, Dad.

"Gianna," My father greeted me in his curt way. "Did you see her?"

Cutting right to the chase.

I raised my chin. "Yes."

He growled. "After I told you not to."

"I'm not a child anymore, Dad, or one of your subordinates. I'm capable of making my own choices."

"What did she want from you?" he asked in a clipped tone.

Surprised by the question, I answered, "Nothing. Why would you ask that?"

"Because that's what she's like." Vitriol twisted his voice.

My patience was already thin. "I understand she left you, and you'll always be bitter, but I need to talk to you about something important. Something—surprising."

"Go ahead."

"My mother did something—magical, I think. It helped me transform." My heart leapt into my throat as I revealed it. "Like her."

Silence.

That was far more unexpected than the shouting I'd expected when I revealed that—his usual way of dealing with me, especially since I'd defied him. I should have Facetimed him to be able to see his expression.

"Dad?"

"Yes."

"Why aren't you saying anything?"

"I'm—I'm—uh—thinking about what you said."

He stuttered? That was atypical of his booming manner. Shouting, yes. Demanding, right. But stuttering? No.

"You know what I mean, right? Her siren form."

"Ah, um, yes. That's surprising."

What was with his odd reaction? Something was off. "Are you sure?"

"Of course, I am."

Pieces started to form abstract shapes in my confused mind. "Have you ever seen me shift before?"

"Gianna, why would you ask that?" The quick way he responded and the higher pitch in his tone was off.

"I had the sense that it wasn't the first time I'd shifted. Dad, tell me the truth. I deserve to hear it."

After a long pause, he exhaled. "Yes."

My mouth widened into an O. "What?"

"Yes," he repeated. "You'd shifted when you were four. I'd taken you to the beach, and you wiggled right out of my arms and swam away. I'd never been so terrified in my life. I didn't think I could get to you. People were around. If they saw you with a tail, it could be dangerous."

More synapses fired in my brain as I tried to process this. Bitterness then coated my tongue. Nova's situation came to mind. Her parents had put a block on her magic when she was young—to keep her safe. Had he done something that nefarious?

In between hastened breaths, I asked. "What. Did. You. Do?"

"What I had to do to protect you."

Blood rushed through my veins, my breath came in jagged bursts. "Tell me. Did you put a block on my magic?"

"What on earth? No. I just scolded you. I yelled at you never to do that again. I was so worried, freaking out, and my shouting terrified you. I felt bad about scaring you, but it was more important to keep you safe."

I blinked twice, my eyelids heavy. "I'd shifted on my own?"

When he didn't respond, I added, "But we'd talked about this when I was little. I asked if I'd grow up to be like my mother and be able to swim like a mermaid. You told me only full sirens had that ability."

"I can't shift." His voice was low. "There are no other sirens in town who could help you. I was barely able to catch up to you when you swam away. You could have gotten into serious danger alone in the ocean. Not only could you get lost, but face predators. You may not understand it, Gianna, but everything I did, I did for your own good. You're my daughter, my only daughter, and I did what I had to care for you the best I could."

My hands trembled. How many times would he repeat what he did was for my own good, to protect me?

"You lied to me."

"I had to."

"Maybe when I was four, but I'm an adult. You don't think you could have ever mentioned it in the twenty-plus years since, that I had the ability to shapeshift?" My voice edged higher, and my hands trembled.

We'd had arguments like this before I'd moved out, more on him forbidding me to do things, and me countering that he couldn't keep me a prisoner. This one was different, though. He'd deceived me. He kept a part of me from myself. That was a form of control I couldn't bear. My heart panged.

"What was the point, Gianna? You lived your life as a human with me."

My skin was covered in a sheen of sweat. "There's more to it, isn't it? You've always hated that side of me, the side that's like my mother. Maybe because it reminds you of her. This is another messed-up instance of trying to control me—to keep me from being like her!"

"Gianna, I told you why. It was to protect you."

"No, it was to protect *you*," I spat. "My mother broke your heart, and you hate any reminder of that. You've been taking it out on me ever since she left us. All the strictness, all the reminders not to be like her."

"It's not like that—"

I cut him off before I burst into tears and shouted things I might regret. "I have to go."

As soon as I hung up the phone, I fell forward with my head into my hands. How could he have lied to me for so long? I pictured myself as a happy four-year-old being shouted at by a huge, tough Marine. No wonder I was terrified and hadn't shifted since.

So many emotions hacked at me, I was surprised I wasn't bleeding all over the sofa. I curled up in the fetal position, trembling as the tears rolled down.

How could I ever trust him again?

SEBASTIAN

While cooking up scallops in lemon and garlic at the restaurant, I thought about Gianna. Was she having a good night at the club?

When Gianna texted me an hour later, asking if I wanted to come over after work, of course I responded yes. Getting through the final hours of my shift then ticked on longer than usual.

When I arrived at her townhouse and knocked on the door, she pulled me inside and kissed me.

"That's the kind of greeting I could get used to," I responded with a grin.

"I want you," she declared and grabbed at me.

Although my body instantly responded to that request, I sensed something was off. I held her upper arms. "Is something wrong?"

"Not now that you're here." She pulled up my shirt and ran her hands up my torso.

She seemed bothered by something, the same as the first night that we'd gone home together.

"Gianna." I pulled my shirt down and caressed her cheek. "If you're upset about something, you can talk to me."

She stared into my eyes. Her lips parted. I thought she was about to reveal what was bothering her.

She bit her lip and then said, "The last thing I want to do right now is talk." She pulled her shirt off, revealing her lush breasts spilling over the cups of her black lacy bra. "Please, Sebastian. I need you." She leaned over and kissed me again.

I couldn't resist my siren's request, not to mention how my wolf was urging me to shut up and take my mate.

That was still an issue. I'd been keeping this from her while expecting her to confide in me. She'd told me about her mother and still I kept this secret. It wasn't right.

While she led me up to her room, I said, "I didn't shower after my shift. I probably stink and should rinse off at least."

"You smell fine to me." She unbuttoned my pants. "But we can start in the shower."

She headed into the bathroom and turned the hot water on. Once we stepped under the waterfall stream, we kissed again, running hands over each other's bodies. I lathered her lush body with soap before sliding inside her from behind. It wasn't the easiest angle, and she propped up her leg on the edge of the tub to help us find a good position.

I reached around to stroke her sensitive nub, and her cries echoed off the tile. When she climaxed with a throaty cry and quivering legs, I followed her into the abyss.

After a brief recovery, we dried each other off and returned to her room for round two. As I thrust inside her, the urge to claim her grew to a feverish peak. I was barely able to keep from exposing my sharpened teeth, ready to mark her as mine.

As we recovered side by side, she turned to me with a relaxed, satiated expression. "That was super hot."

"It always is with you."

She traced her fingers over my chest and smiled. "Now you're the one who looks like they have something on their mind."

My heart still pumping hard, I admitted, "I do."

"What is it?"

This was it. I couldn't keep my secret from her any longer. I rolled onto my side and faced her. "Gianna, there's something I have to tell you."

"Uh oh." She propped herself up on her elbow. "I sense this is serious."

"It is. It means everything to me." I exhaled. "But I don't think you're going to like it."

Her eyes searched mine. "What is it, Sebastian?" Her voice was edged with wariness.

"What my wolf sensed in the beginning… I've since discovered is true."

She narrowed her gaze. "What do you mean?"

I gulped. "You're my mate, Gianna."

She sat up, pulling the sheet over her breasts and let out a nervous laugh. "No. I can't be."

I sat up beside her. "It's true. You're the one for me. The only one."

She shook her head, saying nothing, but breathing hard. After several more seconds, she asked, "How long have you thought this?"

After taking in a heavy breath, I exhaled. "I sensed it the first time we slept together but tried to ignore it. As we spent more time together, it has become vividly clear."

Her bottom lip trembled. "What does this mean? You've been lying to me this entire time?"

"No, I couldn't tell you because…" I motioned to her. "I knew it's not what you wanted.

"Sounds like lying to me." She crossed her arms. "You've been playing with me this whole time, haven't you?"

My eyes widened. "What? Of course not."

She gestured with a harsh wave. "Just stringing me along. Pretending to be casual. It was all faked, so you could trick me into being with you!"

I expected her to react strongly, but accuse me like this? "No, Gianna. Listen to me."

"No, I won't." She climbed out of bed and pulled on her panties. "You're just as bad as him."

"Who?" I stood and found my boxer shorts, putting them on.

She yanked a faded, oversized Whitesnake T-shirt over her head. "My father."

I blinked at her. "Your father?" Where did this come from and what the hell was going on? "Why are you comparing me to him?"

"You deceived me. Just like he has. You're trying to get me to fall for you, knowing I don't want this." She motioned between us.

Frustration churned, and I grasped my hair. "That's exactly why I didn't push it," I exploded. "I was trying to respect your damn wishes!"

"What?" she stared at me with a perplexed expression.

"How do you think it feels to want someone so badly? To think she cares somewhat for you, or at least wants to sleep with you. But you're unable to talk about it with her because you know it might upset her. I've kept my feelings to myself for you."

"This is too much." She raised both hands to the sides of her head. "I can't deal with another lie. I can't handle one more thing in my screwed-up life right now. Please go." She pointed to her bedroom door.

"Don't do this," I said.

"Sebastian..." Her chest rose and fell with escalated breaths.

"Damn it, Gianna. All I want to do is care for you and protect you. Don't push me away."

She brought her fingers in between her brows. "Oh my God. Not this, too."

"Not what?"

She shook her hands. "You're just like him. Why do you think I need to be taken care of? Protected? I've been taking care of myself for a long damn time now." She pointed at me. "And don't you dare say it's what's best for me because how the hell do you know?"

Aware that I was standing there like an idiot in my boxers while she yelled at me, I found the sense to pull on my clothes. "Why are you freaking out? I thought we were friends at the very least."

She sneered. "Friends don't lie—and try to control each other."

"I'm not trying to control you," I protested.

"You are," she snapped. "By saying I'm your mate. I'm not yours. I'm not anyone's to have and control!"

"Holy fuck, Gianna!" I strode over to her in two steps and took her raised arm by the wrist. "Do you think I planned this? That I'd be crazy enough to choose to fall for someone who doesn't want what I ache for with every part of my being?"

"And what's that?"

"To be with you."

We stared at each other, faces inches apart. The only sound was our rapid breathing. I released her arm.

The anger flashing in her eyes was replaced by a glimpse of vulnerability. Was I finally—*finally*—breaking through?

"I'm not the right woman for you, Sebastian. You deserve someone much better than me." She stepped to the side. "Someone without all my issues."

"I don't want anyone else. I only want you."

A strangled sound escaped her. "That's the problem."

"Why?"

"Because I'm not able to commit to anyone."

"Why do you think that? Because you're half-siren?" I asked.

She pursed her lips and averted my gaze. "Yes."

"Bullshit," I spat.

"What?" She stared at me with an incredulous expression.

"You use that as a shield, as an excuse not to get too close to anyone. Why? Is it because you're afraid of getting hurt? Afraid of someone leaving you again?"

Her face crumbled. She appeared on the verge of breaking.

"I would never do that to you, Gianna. Can't you see how right we are for each other?" I stepped closer to her, covering my heart. "I'd never hurt you. Never leave you. You're the only one for me."

"Stop it, stop it." She rushed out the bedroom door.

I grabbed my shirt and pulled it on as I followed her down the stairs and into the living room. "You might not want to hear it, but you know it's true. You know you have feelings for me, but you're just too afraid to admit it."

She turned, snapping a neutral mask back in place. "The sex was great, Sebastian," she said in a tone much cooler and controlled than the emotional one upstairs. "But that's all it was. We're not Nova and Diego and can never be in a relationship like them."

"You're wrong." I raised my index finger and stepped closer. "It was never just sex, and you know it."

She moved to the door and opened it. "You have to leave."

"Gianna."

"Go," she insisted. "It's over."

My heartbeat thundered in my ears, and my head felt dizzy. Her words echoed in my head, cutting with a vicious bite with each repetition.

Any hope that I'd harbored, thinking I might be breaking through, vanished. I walked out of the front door like a ghost.

When she closed the door behind me, the greatest fear of any shifter slithered under my skin. It was worse than my phobia of water. Worse than anything I could imagine, wringing me so cold that it shook me deep into my bones.

My mate rejected me.

CHAPTER 14

GIANNA

After Sebastian left, I leaned against the door, body quaking. I never should have called him after being upset about my father. With the way that Sebastian had such a wonderful manner of comforting and caring for me, he'd been the first to come to mind.

But then it imploded.

He'd lied to me. Or, at the very least, kept something extremely important from me. Same thing, right?

A shaky sob tore through me. I inhaled a shuddering breath.

Why had I let things go so far? It was stupid and reckless to even play around and then get involved with him when I was such a wreck. A hot freaking mess.

Mates, what did that even mean? A commitment for life? I couldn't even commit to a long-term relationship.

Sebastian's face fell, and a part of me wished I snapped it all back. But why? What I said was true, it would never work out. He was better off with someone who could give him what he wanted. Someone better than me, without all my issues. I was better off with someone who didn't want anything from me.

Jakob came to mind. Right. Nothing serious, just short-term fun. We'd get together and go our own ways, and nobody would get hurt.

Like I'd hurt Sebastian.

The way he'd looked at me when I'd ended it, so lost and vulnerable, almost made me relent. Why did I have to be such a cold bitch? He deserved better, so much better. Part of me had started to crumble thinking about running into his arms and telling him I wanted to be with him, too.

But he'd deceived me.

Right. Self-preservation kicked in.

If I allowed a man to lie and control me the way my father had, then I'd be wrapping chains around myself. I'd be responsible for my own self-destruction.

I'd survived on my own. Why change? So I could be controlled by another man? No way. Never.

If that was what a relationship was, I wanted no part of it.

But Sebastian had never tried to control me. I softened. Maybe we should talk this out…

The urge to open the door and call him back inside rose. Before I did something stupid, like act on it, I forced myself to walk away.

SEBASTIAN

Rejected.

That word echoed in my head with vicious mockery as I walked away from Gianna's. It didn't matter that I'd left the pack—its shackles caught up with me in the end. This wasn't just any woman who rejected me but my mate.

Everything I'd ever feared about that concept came to fruition with Gianna's cutting words. It was over. We were done.

My wolf howled inside in anguish. I felt the same way.

Once I drove home and entered the house, I was ready to curl up on the ground and lick my wounds.

Lucas glanced up from the video game he was playing. "You all right, man? You look like a lost ghost."

I shook my head and sank onto the sofa. A hint of Gianna's scent lingered to torment me. How long before it faded? "My mate rejected me."

"No..." Lucas paused the game and stared at me in doubt. "Gianna?" His eyes widened.

I nodded. "Yes."

"I thought you said it was a false alarm. That your wolf was confused by her siren mojo or what not."

My mouth curled into a scowl. "I was hoping that was true. It turned out it wasn't."

Lucas put the game remote down. "Women are trouble. You know that." He raised his chin. "Come out with me tomorrow night." He arched a brow. "We'll find new trouble to take your mind of her."

I scowled. "No. I'm not in the mood."

"What are you in the mood for?" he asked.

"Nothing. No one."

"Sebastian," Lucas prodded. "Are you okay?"

Could I sound any more morose? "I have to work tonight," I explained. "And then I'll let my wolf run to get some of this out. The last thing I need is to be around people."

Lucas stood and patted me on the back. "Okay, man. If you change your mind, you know where to find me."

I didn't. I wouldn't.

WHILE AT THE RESTAURANT, I avoided my coworkers and focused on prepping meals.

"You're unusually quiet tonight," one of the servers noted.

That was true. I loved my job and often chatted with others while I worked. Tonight, I kept to myself so I wouldn't lash out at some innocent bystander.

"I'm having a bad day," I explained. Hopefully, that would give her the hint to tell everyone to stay far, far away.

While I cooked steaks and seafood, I reprimanded myself for being such a fool. I should have known this would happen. Gianna had made her feelings clear from the start. Yet, what did I do—pursued and wooed. For what? To convince her of what she told me straight out she didn't want? Stupid. Foolish. I was an idiot and deserved exactly what I'd gotten.

If my pack could see me now, they'd laugh—even more so when I was the small, weak pup they'd picked on. Maybe they were right, I had nothing to offer anyone of value. I was a pathetic shifter pining after a woman who could never love me.

I was a joke.

No matter how far I ran and reinvented my life, the pack won in the end.

The hours until the restaurant closed dragged on, the din of people laughing and having fun grating. Once able to leave, I sped to the woods, searching for a secluded parking spot. After I parked and trudged into the woods, I shifted into wolf form and ran up the hill. My wolf ran with a restlessness, but this time it was different. He wasn't eager to pursue our newly discovered mate but run from the anguish of losing her.

I was being punished for leaving my pack, that had to be it. Since I'd left, the universe decided to show me what rejection truly felt like, pairing me with a mate who'd reject me in turn.

My desperate wolf ran to the top of the hill and howled in anguish. This was fucking unbearable. The ache of loss vibrated deep into my soul.

GIANNA

THE MORNING after I'd ended it with Sebastian, I woke up feeling weighed down with despair. Why couldn't I have been able to reciprocate his feelings? We could have been happy, right?

Wrong. I was too different. Too screwed up.

After a cup of hot coffee, I called Nova to tell her what happened.

"I'm sorry," she said. "How are you doing?"

"Miserable." I huffed. "Confused."

"About?"

"Since New Year's Eve, I'd say about everything." All the chaos in my brain started when my mother had returned.

"Right, the night your mother returned."

"That's the thing. I think I should go stay with her for a bit. Find out who I truly am."

"Gianna, you know who you are. It doesn't matter if you're part this or half that. You're you, and that's what makes you incredible."

I smiled. "Thanks. I needed to hear that. Especially as I'm feeling like shit." I took a deep breath and exhaled. "But I'm still going to stay with her and just—see."

When I returned to the beach house, my mother opened the door, looking stunning in a red-flowered sarong. Her hair fell in loose waves over her shoulders as if sun-dried after a swim.

"Gianna, I'm so glad you decided to return." She stepped aside so I could enter. "Come in."

Once back in the family room that went overboard with the seaside decor, I babbled a condensed version to her. "This shifter I've been kind of seeing thinks I'm his mate—not just his wolf." I exhaled and raised my chin. "But I'm not. I can't be." I peered at her. "Right?"

With a dismissive wave, she said, "Forget him. He's not right for you, nor you for him."

I bristled. Was that true? I shook my head. Of course it was.

Then why did hearing her say it bother me?

"You're with us now. You're one of us."

Right, that's why I came here, I reminded myself—to find others like me. To find where I truly belonged.

"You know what they say about fish in the sea. Once you find a new lover, you'll forget that furry canine." She rolled one shoulder and motioned with her hand. "Take Jakob. He'd be perfect. No expectations. No promises."

No one getting hurt.

That would be welcome. I hated how I treated Sebastian and hated how I felt. Not being tormented by the constant questions of my choices would be a welcome break.

"Maybe."

Jakob was hotter than fire in a cauldron. Why wasn't I more excited about this prospect? I should be eager to climb up his body and slide down like a fire pole.

Sebastian's face popped into mind with his warm brown eyes that burned gold with hunger when he wanted me. Damn. Had he ruined me from enjoying other men?

No, I'd force myself to move on. Fake it 'til you make it.

With what—orgasms?

"Come on," my mother said. "Let's go swim."

SWIMMING with the pod in siren form was the same surreal experience as last time, but I knew what to expect. I lost track of time as we swam in the harbor. Jakob brushed his tail against mine as he glided past. Then he darted around me, chasing me in a sort of underwater flirtation. Although captivated by this underwater world with sea plants and varied hues of fish, I wasn't sure how I felt about Jakob's attention. Yes, he was gorgeous and sleek and had the perfect male body, even in this tailed form. Yet I wasn't as onboard as I'd expect myself to be.

Once we returned inside the beach house, back in human forms, he remained by my side, touching me often.

After we ate takeout from a local seafood restaurant, Jakob took my hand. "Come with me, Gianna."

I accepted his hand, interested to see what he had in mind. He led me upstairs to his room. Once he closed the door, he bent down to kiss me.

"No." I pulled my head away before I realized what I was doing.

Why was I turning this gorgeous, god-level attractive man away? This wasn't some mortal who I attempted to pick up in a club. This was someone powerful and compelling and I should be heady with desire.

"No?" he pulled back and brought his brows closer.

He'd probably never been turned down by anyone in his life.

I stared at him, gazing at his perfect bone structure like it was alien. Nothing. No burning desire. Something about it seemed shallow and without substance.

Ugh, I never wanted something substantial before. What was wrong with me?

"Sorry, it just—doesn't feel right." I shook my head and rubbed my forehead. "Not yet, at least."

Not like with Sebastian, when every part of me was drawn to him and every particle in my body responded with eager expectation. What was going on? I couldn't continue like this. I was better suited with someone like Jakob.

Wasn't I?

Then why didn't I feel any sort of connection, not like that undeniable lure to Sebastian?

After slipping away from Jakob, I returned to my room—alone.

THE NEXT MORNING, I woke as the sun rose. While the house was quiet with everyone still asleep, I dressed and quietly stepped outside the French door with a blanket. I set it down on the sand and watched the sea birds as they swooped in searching for food. They sang, greeting the new day under the gleaming sun. The light rippled on the ocean's surface as the waves rolled in and out from the shore, lulling me with their soothing sound.

Being here with my mother had answered some questions and raised more. I didn't yet know what to do with what I'd learned.

Everyone else was back in the house, likely still asleep. I pictured Jakob and his model-perfect beauty. He'd beckoned me to go to his room with him last night, but I couldn't. I'd said I wasn't ready.

Not ready? I was usually the one leading the seduction.

I had to go back to the way I was before—having fun, avoiding relationships, and keeping my life simple.

Before Sebastian.

That way I wouldn't have to deal with these confusing, unfamiliar feelings. Sure, I'd felt wonderful around him. It felt good to be wanted and cared for. To have someone think of you in a much more positive light than you ever thought of yourself. Even his crazy possessive, protective streak had started to grow on me.

But mates? Meaning—*forever?*

That was insane. Terrifying. I had to put it out my mind.

THAT AFTERNOON, I went for a walk on the beach with my mother. The ocean breeze was strong enough that it snapped our hair around our face at times.

After we spoke about innocuous observations of the weather, she asked, "Who do you spend your time with when you're not working?"

I grimaced. Lately, it had been with Sebastian until that had fallen apart. "I often hung out with staff at the club, but my friend Nova returned to Salem recently, so we've been spending more time together."

"Tell me about her."

I shrugged. "She's petite, has auburn hair, and is a witch. Only she couldn't do magic until recently."

"Why is that?"

"Oh, it's a long story." I brushed it off with a wave.

"I have time," she replied.

"Not much to tell. She didn't think she could do magic." I shrugged.

"I wonder why," my mother asked, interest gleaming in her eyes.

A pang of hurt churned inside. Why was my mother more interested in Nova's magical abilities than my own? Something was off. Was it weird jealously on my part or something else?

"No idea," I lied.

"Oh, surely you do," my mom persisted with a tap on my arm and a persuasive smile.

The bullshit radar was up and engaged. "Why are you so interested in my friend's magical ability?"

"I'm a siren. Naturally, I'm interested in magic."

Was that a natural interest for sirens? Maybe I was being far too sensitive because my mother asked an innocent question about my friend. This was a typical mom question, right? It wouldn't be the suspicious scrutiny that my father had often adopted. *Who are you going to be with? Where are you going?*

"We're in Salem. There are plenty of witches here, so plenty of magic. Her aunt had been persuaded to put a block on Nova's abilities when she was little, and she wasn't aware she could use magic until her aunt died."

"Fascinating," my mother said with a gleam in her eye.

Once again, a pang of jealously twisted inside. Couldn't she show more interest in me?

AFTER SPENDING another night in the beach house, evading Jakob's attempts to get together once more, I lay alone in my bed and thought of Sebastian. I hadn't been able to shake the yearning to be with him.

A part of me longed to see him again. To care for and protect him the way he'd often done for me. To shield him from the pain I'd caused him—and myself.

My heart thumped. What had he done to me? Did he make me feel—*like him?*

No, no, no. I rolled onto my side, covering my head as if I could force my feelings away. What were these emotions? And what the hell was I supposed to do with them?

Could it be—love?

I shook my head. Why would I think that now while I was here trying to explore my siren side? Maybe I'd decide to leave Salem and swim away with my mother and her pod. We could be adventurous and free, living without complications.

I frowned. It would also mean leaving everything and everyone behind. I'd worked so hard to build up the Danger Zone and buy my townhouse. Was I ready to give those up?

No. Maybe I was more attached to my life in Salem here than I realized. I had good people in my life, good friends.

Before I made any rash decisions, I had to sleep on it.

THE NEXT MORNING, I woke in the now familiar beach-themed bedroom. It wasn't my bed. I missed my room.

I pulled out my phone and texted Nova. *Things are weird here. How are you doing?*

Fine. Weird how?

Not exactly sure. I thought I'd find where I'd belong here. Now I'm not so sure.

You're always part of my tribe.

When she added a silly emoji, I laughed. *I know.*

How long are you staying? Nova asked.

Good question. Did I have any reason to stay? I went through the reasons why I'd come here. I'd wanted to learn more about my siren side and myself. I thought I'd fit better in this world with others like me. That didn't appear to be the case. In fact, I felt more connected to the hodgepodge supernatural crew that lived under Nova's roof than I did here.

Specifically with the wolf shifter who thought I was his mate.

Maybe I'd come here to run away from my true feelings.

I was afraid. Afraid of feelings so strong, which I'd never felt before. I was a coward to have pushed him away instead of facing my fears. Hadn't I been the one to encourage him to face his own in joining me in the pool? If he could take on that long-standing phobia with me, I could summon the courage to face my issues with abandonment and commitment and control with him.

Oh, this poor shifter didn't realize he'd have his hands full falling for someone like me.

I'm coming back today, I texted Nova. *I need to talk to Sebastian. Maybe we can see if we can find a way to make this work.*

Yes! she replied and added a half-dozen smiley faces with heart eyes. *Good for you.*

I then texted Sebastian, my pulse firing more rapidly as I typed. *Can we talk later?*

While I awaited his reply, my leg twitched. Would he even want anything to do with me after the way I'd treated him?

Of course, he replied. *When and where?*

I exhaled a deep sigh of relief. *Eight. My place?*

See you then.

I closed my eyes. Amid all my confusion of late, a new lightness filled me. I was going home.

CHAPTER 15

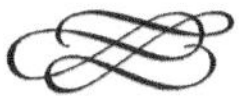

GIANNA

Since this would be my last day with the pod, I hung out at the beach house with them. Part of me wanted to ensure I was doing the right thing, what I wanted. The more time I spent with them, the more I realized I didn't have much in common with them—especially with all the wariness and whispers. Whatever they discussed, they didn't want me to know.

That afternoon, I found my mother. "Thanks for letting me stay here. It's time I go back home."

She frowned. "You can't leave already."

"Why not?"

"We have so much to talk about. So much to prepare."

I furrowed my brows. "What are you talking about?"

"Sit down, Gianna." She brushed my arm.

"Okay."

"We need you, Gianna. We need your help to find a portal."

I blinked at her. "A what?"

"The portal where Max and Jakob came through many years ago."

My gut churned. "They came from—another world?"

She sighed. "You don't know much about the magical world, do you?"

I mashed my lips together before I spat something caustic, blaming her once more. "Not what you're talking about."

"A portal will open soon. We need to help others like Max and Jakob through."

"What are they?" The question that still hadn't been answered. "Why do they look like sirens when they swim?"

She brought her long, slender fingertips together. "They're able to take on whatever form they like. Part of their magic."

That could mean they were shifters, like Sebastian. Or worse.

Much much worse.

"Please tell me they're not demons," I said.

"What if they are?" She rolled a shoulder, as if it meant nothing.

Terror clamped around my throat. My skin turned clammy. Demons.

"Just as sirens have been smeared as monsters over the centuries, so have demons."

I blinked, trying to follow along with the logic.

Maybe that was possible, except the one I'd encountered one was truly monstrous in my eyes. "One kidnapped me not to long ago. He was terrible. Exploiting me to gain access to power."

My mother seemed unfazed by it. Her expression, not changing. Did she not give a shit about my trauma?

"With all the magic in this town, we need to be the ones in power and control the portal." She gestured at me. "That's why we need you to talk to your friend, Nova."

My eyes widened. "Is that what your interest was in Nova?"

"She's a witch. She works for the Network. She's your friend. Naturally, we could use your connection to find out more."

Lowering my head into my hands, I said, "I don't believe this."

"Get her to come here and join us. We can all work together, and then we'll rule Salem."

My gut sank to the hardwood floor. I raised my gaze to meet hers, which now had a wild spark.

"You're connected to the attempt to infiltrate the Network, aren't you?" I accused.

She scowled, twisting her features. "They had it well protected with magic. That's why we need an insider like your friend."

I stepped back. "You didn't want to get to know me at all. You were just using me."

"Don't be so dramatic, Gianna. We're talking incredible power."

If I thought my father had been triggering, my mother who had rejected me my entire life telling me I was dramatic was like slamming on a big red button on my back.

It all came together. My father's warning. My mother's peculiar interest in Nova. My wounds had left me blind to the truth.

I'd wanted so much to know and understand this other world that I hadn't grown up in, or a part of, with a mother who'd always been a mythical figure, that I'd avoided the warning signs.

"I don't want power. All I wanted was a mother. But not like this." I backed up. She was cold and detached and incapable of love, like my father had warned. She was using me. "You never cared for me, did you? It was all part of this power trip or whatever you seek."

"I told you our ways aren't like humans." She sneered with disdain. "Maybe you're more human than you think."

Her words dawned on me. "Yes, that's right. I'd been raised by my father. Even if he was strict and controlling, he cared about me and loved me. He'd do anything to protect me. That's more than you've ever done."

"Are you finished now?" she asked with dire exasperation. "I'm offering you the chance of a lifetime. The portal only opens on rare occasions. We must meet those coming through."

"Demons." I scowled, the word left a foul taste on my tongue.

"We need to recruit them to our side," she said. "With their numbers and abilities, we will be able to seize control. All the magic you ever dreamed about will be possible once we control this town and all the magic within it. We will be formidable."

Where did this power-hungry persona come from? Who was this bitch who gave birth to me?

"No way." I shook my fist. "Absolutely not."

"Don't be foolish, Gianna. I'm offering you something beyond your wildest dreams."

"Then you don't know me at all." I continued to move backwards, desperate to get away from her. "I've never dreamed of that, and I don't want anything to do with it. I dreamed of having a normal family, a kind mother."

"Enough whining," she snapped. "We have work to do." She pointed at me. "Tell me everything you know about the Network."

"I'm not telling you shit." I turned to leave, but she grabbed my wrist, and holy hell, she had a strong grip.

"I wish you'd never come here. Get out of my life. Get out of this city. I never want to see you again."

She grabbed my arm and stopped me. "You will if you know what's best for you."

Her sharp tone was just as formidable as her physical strength. I turned with wariness. Her expression was cold. All my life I'd wondered what she was like. Knowing her was far worse.

"Are you that much of a monster that you'd threaten your daughter?"

"I'm giving you the chance for an incredible opportunity to join us, and like an ungrateful child, you sulk about the past. Grow up and get over it."

Her words hit me as more vicious than a slap. "You don't get to scold me. You lost the right when you walked away, abandoning all parental responsibilities."

"I've heard enough of your complaints," she snarled. "Jakob," she shouted.

When he entered the room, she said, "She's not cooperating. Do what you will to get the information we need."

Jakob smirked as he sauntered over. He ran one cold finger down the side of my face and down my neck. "With pleasure."

I turned my face away from him in repulsion. "Don't touch me."

"I'll do whatever I want with you." He grabbed my wrists and pinned them behind my back with quick force before I even had a chance to react.

"I have rope," Max said.

I turned to see my mother's lover helping Jakob bind my arms behind me. I struggled, but it was no use. They were both too powerful.

Max stepped back and stroked his chin, like some caricature of a villain concocting an evil plan. "Find out how her witch friend was able to defeat Andre."

Andre—that demon who had kidnapped me. "You were working with that monster?"

Jakob sneered. He bent down and licked my face. "Don't worry, you'll like me better than that shaggy wolf you've been fucking. Demons do everything better."

I gagged at the cold wetness of his vile tongue on my skin. "Eww." I shuddered. "Keep that disgusting tongue off of me, or I'll find a way to rip it out of your skull!"

Jakob dropped his head back and laughed—one with such a malevolent undertone that I shivered. "I love your spunk, siren." He ran his finger down my shoulder and over my breast. "And I will greatly enjoy getting information out of you—no matter how long it takes." He flashed an evil, mirthless smile. "Or how deep I have to penetrate to break you."

Icy terror swirled like mist from my ankles and up my spine. I held my chin up, refusing to let this creature see how he terrified me.

"Want me to help?" Max asked.

"No, I'm going to enjoy this on my own." He circled around me and sniffed. "Her fear is intoxicating."

I gritted my jaw.

Max said, "Enjoy," and then left the room.

My mother said, "Better yet, get her to lure her witch friend here. We can force her to give us information."

No, not again. That demon Andre had used me to get Nova to bring her family's Book of Shadows to him. Now these demons were going to use me as bait once more? No matter what they did, I wouldn't let it happen.

No matter what.

My mother left the room, leaving me alone with this demon. How could I ever have considered being with Jakob? Everything about him was vile and turned me off.

So much regret rose. Had I been so blind by my desperation to know my mother that I'd pushed away those who truly cared for me?

One person came to mind above all. He'd shielded his true feelings because of how I'd react. Sebastian had done nothing but try to protect me and keep me happy. He'd been so considerate, never asking for more than I could give, and like a fool, I'd pushed him away.

I struggled against the rope restraining my wrists. No use.

In the end, by trying to shield myself from pain, I'd locked the constraints around myself. My wounds kept me from pursuing happiness, which was something I had a glimpse of with Sebastian. He'd patiently waited for me to wake up and see what had been clear to him from the first moment we met—we were meant to be together.

Too bad, I was a jaded jackass and couldn't see what was best for me. Instead, I followed down this dark path leading to destruction. Dragging me into my worst nightmares.

"Splendid, this is what you fear most." Jakob's eyes widened with a combination of delight and surprise. "Restraint."

Shit, was he reading my mind?

"I sense your fear." He sniffed my neck. "It energizes me."

"Get the fuck away from me!" I spat and tried to escape the ropes binding me one more time. My breathing escalated and my heartbeat clamored as I struggled to get out.

He laughed. "You should know by now that it won't work. And the greater your terror, the higher my enjoyment."

I growled in frustration and then stopped the futile struggle. Was there any way I could escape this nightmare? My mind flashed with one horrifying instance after another of how a demon might torture me. Binding me and removing all my control would be vicious torment in itself. And then, he'd do the same to Nova.

I forced the images away, they would only escalate my horror—and give him fuel on how to break me.

"Keep it going," he drawled with delight. "Tell me all your delicious fears."

I was caught in my worst nightmare of being locked up, only this time it wasn't just one demon, but two.

And the one who had done this to me was my own mother.

I screamed for help.

"Sing for me, siren." Jakob laughed. "Eventually you'll sing the song I want to hear."

CHAPTER 16

SEBASTIAN

ianna's car wasn't at her townhouse. I was five minutes early, so I stayed in my car to wait. I listened to music and scrolled through social media to kill time.

Eight o'clock came. Eight went. Fifteen more minutes went by. Maybe she was running late. I didn't want to bother her, but at twenty past, I texted her.

With no answer by eight-thirty, my worries rose. I called, and she didn't answer. My wolf was antsy inside. The promise of seeing our mate again foiled by her not being there.

Look for her, he urged.

In agreement, I started by calling Nova. Once she answered, I burst right into my concerns. "Gianna was supposed to meet me at her townhouse a half-an-hour ago. Maybe I'm being too antsy, but I'm worried."

"Oh," Nova said, her voice sinking.

"What?"

"She was at the beach house with her mother. She might have gotten held up."

Despite her words, I sensed a twinge of concern in her voice. "What's up, Nova?"

"What do you mean?"

"I hear the worry in your tone."

"It's just—I don't know, Sebastian. Something about this whole thing with her mother doesn't sit right with me. Gianna said it was weird there, and she was ready to leave."

I stood straighter. "Do you think she's in trouble?"

"No, I didn't say that—"

"What's the address?"

"Sebastian, what are you planning on doing?"

"Going to make sure she's safe."

Nova sighed. "She might be pissed if you show up, but I'm a little worried myself. I'll go with you. At least, she won't just lash out at you—"

"What's the address?" I cut Nova off.

Once she gave it to me, she asked, "Do you want to pick me up so we can go together?"

"No time, Nova. I'm going now." I ended the call.

I sped down to the location near the harbor. Only while driving did Nova's words sink in. Gianna might be pissed at me interfering in her life this way. Damn it, I couldn't sit back knowing something might be off. She was supposed to meet me, and she didn't. Maybe she'd lost track of time with her mother.

Or maybe...

I couldn't think it. The idea of Gianna in danger ripped a hole inside.

Nova called back as I parked on the side of the road in front of the address of the weathered beach house. Gianna's red coupe was parked in the driveway.

"I just pulled up to the beach house," I told her. "Gianna's car is here."

"Sebastian, please don't go in alone," Nova warned. "I talked to Zoe. We're coming down to investigate. She said there's some evidence to link those staying there to the attempt at infiltrating the Network."

"And Gianna's in there alone with them." I climbed out of the car and hurried up the walkway. "I'm going to check on her now."

"Sebastian, wait for us. You don't know if they're dangerous."

"Or if Gianna's in danger," I added. "No way in hell am I going to wait to find out."

I ended the call. My wolf pushed me to burst through the front door and protect our mate.

Calm down, I urged. *We don't know the situation. There might be nothing to fear.*

My words seemed hollow. Something felt wrong, and I wouldn't rest easy until I saw that Gianna was okay.

I knocked on the door. After I counted to thirty with no reply, I pounded on it some more.

A man answered. He stood well over six-feet tall with blond hair and appraised me from cold eyes. His scent wasn't that of a human but not one I could identify either.

"I'm here to see Gianna," I said without any introduction.

This dude raised a brow and then sniffed. "She's unavailable, wolf." He pushed the door closed.

I put my foot in the doorway, preventing him from shutting the door. So, he knew what I was. "I'm not leaving until I see her."

He narrowed his cold eyes with amusement. "That's not going to happen."

My wolf growled, his shoulders rising at this man he perceived as a threat.

Yes, we're going after her, I promised. I wouldn't leave without making sure she was okay. I didn't care if she damned me to hell and cursed me out. She'd already done that. What did I have to lose? I'd already lost her, but that didn't mean I wouldn't fight like hell to protect her.

"Where is she?" Without waiting for a reply, I pushed the door open. "Gianna!"

GIANNA

Sebastian?

It couldn't be him here, now, could it? Was it this demon screwing with my head?

Jakob had dragged me to the back of the house and tied me to the handles of the French doors. He then detailed all the vile things he wanted to do to torment me, escalating my terror for his perverse pleasure.

"Sebastian, I'm in here!" My throat burned. I'd screamed for help until it had turned raw.

Jakob grabbed my neck, increasing the pain. He seethed as he glared at me. "Careful, siren. You don't want to piss me off."

Or what, he'd torture me? He'd already outlined that in excruciating detail, relishing how it made me perspire. He even licked my puckered goose flesh. Ewww. I shuddered once more.

He tightened his hold, so I couldn't respond with something snarky—even if I'd thought of a good comeback. Instead, I gasped for breath.

The door splintered into the room like it had been exploded. Sebastian kicked it in and stepped inside. His eyes glowed with feral anger.

If I wasn't restrained, I'd hug him. I'd never been so happy to see anyone, ever.

The brown of his eyes glowed a fierce amber. When his gaze locked on mine, my heart quickened. He came for me.

He turned to Jakob. "Let go of her now," he demanded in a low, dangerous tone that promised retribution to anyone who refused him.

Jakob stepped in front of me and snarled. "You must be the wolf she's been screwing." He flared his nostrils. "Making her smell like wet dog."

Sebastian growled in response.

"She's moved on to bigger—and better," Jakob mocked.

Sebastian's expression turned feral, reminding me of the first time I'd seen him like this in the club, but far more dangerous.

"Don't listen to him," I croaked, my voice hoarse from Jakob's pressure on my neck. "He's lying."

Sebastian widened his stance and circled before Jakob. With his shoulders raised and arms wider, he appeared larger and broader. A virulent, sexy predator.

"Untie her or get the hell out of my way," Sebastian seethed. A low warning groan followed that seemed to vibrate from deep within his chest.

With his dominant stance and determined glare, as if ready to tear into anyone to protect me, I'd never been more drawn to him—or anyone. He was the hottest fuckin' being I'd ever seen.

Jakob dropped his head back and sniffed. "I smell your fear, little wolf." His lips curled into a sneer.

Max entered the room and assessed the scene.

"Yes, I'll untie her," Jakob agreed.

Wait, what? Something was up. Why would Jakob suddenly cooperate?

"Sebastian, be careful," I warned.

Of what, I didn't know. In the next heartbeat, a flash of brightness blinded me, followed by smoke. I choked on the cloying scent, and it scratched at my already raw throat. Someone worked on the rope, untying me from the door handles and then dragged me outside. My heart leaped with relief. Sebastian must have gotten to me.

The rough yanking wasn't like Sebastian's gentle touch. When my vision cleared, my gut dropped. It wasn't Sebastian, but Jakob. He and Max were outside, dragging me to the dock. That's when I realized my wrists were still bound—and Sebastian was on the floor inside, choking.

"What did you do?" I cried. My attempt to claw at Jakob failed, so I tried to kick him. At least my legs weren't bound.

He evaded my kicks and laughed. "You sheltered siren. Haven't you ever encountered dark magic?"

Sebastian brought himself to his feet, dragging himself forward as he coughed and gasped for breath.

His body shimmered and vibrated as he rushed out the open doors toward us.

"Let's go, wolf," Jakob taunted as he ran toward Sebastian.

Gray fur sprouted from his body. As he leapt, his body shifted shape, contorting to a four-legged form covered in gray fur. When he landed on Jakob on the sand, Sebastian was fully in wolf form.

As they rolled on the ground, electric blue sparks shot from Jakob's hands. Sebastian gnashed at Jakob. A spurt of blood sprayed out, marring Sebastian's beautiful fur.

"Sebastian!" I cried out.

Max dragged me down the dock out over the harbor.

"Where are you taking me?" I demanded.

"Shut up."

Headlights passed by my eyes, blinding me momentarily, as two cars pulled up.

"Shit, they've found us," Max shouted at Jakob.

Who?

"Get rid of her," Jakob shouted while grappling with Sebastian.

Sebastian growled and attacked Jakob with more frenzy.

Max led me farther down the dock. He looped an anchor tied to a rope around me and taunted, "How tragic that a big, bad wolf afraid of water falls for a siren."

Jakob pulled away from Sebastian and laughed. "Just like in those old tales, she'll lure you to a watery grave."

Sebastian ran to us. But not before Jakob dragged me to the edge of the dock and threw me into the dark water.

SEBASTIAN

After that monster threw Gianna into the harbor, I ran after her. This other damn one I'd been fighting tackled me. As we rolled on the dock, my head mere inches from the dark water, ice froze my veins.

The sea. A watery grave, just as he'd taunted. My utmost fear.

Figures approached, coming toward the dock shouting at us to stop.

"Let's go, Jakob," the one who'd thrown Gianna commanded. "Leave him for another time."

With crimson eyes and vicious fangs, this Jakob dude continued to parry.

"This isn't the time. We need more to fight them," the older guy commanded before he dove into the water.

Who?

Jakob stole a quick glance behind me at the figures and then at the water. "Do you dare come after us, little wolf," Jakob mocked with a sneer before he leapt in.

I stared at the rippling surface of the dark water where they'd gone under, and my muscles hardened. My fur stood on end in the cool winter air. I had to get to Gianna, but I froze. All the memories of being a young pup rushed back in a flood. Falling under through the ice and struggling not to drown. The torment that had followed when older pack mates held me under water. All of it played in my head like a fast-motioned horror film, paralyzing me.

My wolf was just as fearful, conflicted between rescuing our mate and the terror of drowning.

Gianna was under there. Restrained. I had to face this fear and get to her. Had to. There was no choice. It was Gianna or nothing at all.

The voices that approached were muffled as I struggled to summon enough courage to face this lifelong terror.

Forget those other times. Think of the time in the pool with Gianna.

She'd stayed with me there, holding my hands, distracting me with sensual promises and soothing me with sweet comfort until the petrification passed.

Wait, this wasn't my greatest fear. It wasn't drowning or even being rejected by my mate. It was losing Gianna.

Yes, I could face this. I'd do whatever I had to do to save her.

Shifting back to human form so I'd have use of my hands, I took a giant inhale and dove into water. The frigid water hit me like a brutal slap. Forcing myself to ignore the sting on my flesh and saltwater burning my eyes, I swam down and searched for Gianna.

Ahead the two male beings had shifted into a tailed form and swam ahead. Several women with tails shimmered in the distance. Momentarily stunned by seeing beings like this, I stared in awe.

Movement below snapped me from my spell. A woman with long dark hair and a turquoise iridescent tail struggled near the bottom. It was Gianna!

I swam down, using all my willpower and strength to fight against the urge to resurface.

When I touched her bound arms, attempting to help her, she gnashed around with fierceness as if trying to defend herself.

Shit. This was bad. I couldn't free her if she thought I was there to attack her.

I wanted to talk, to tell her that it was me, but couldn't beneath the water. The pressure on my lungs grew more intense.

She stopped fighting. She must have realized it was me.

I unwrapped the anchored rope from around her lower body, mesmerized by her stunning tail. When I'd finally removed it, I reached for the rope binding her wrists behind her back. This wasn't as easy as the knots were fastened tight.

Precious seconds ticked me as a panicky sensation rose. I forced myself to keep going, to keep at it to free Gianna, while my vision narrowed.

Finally, finally, the rope fell from her arms.

But it was too late. The blackness closed in.

Swallowing me.

CHAPTER 17

GIANNA

Sebastian had to be okay. He had to be.

I held his limp body as I swam to the surface, swishing my tail to get us there quicker.

I didn't know he'd been there, trying to help me. Jakob and Max had left me, swimming ahead to meet up with the pod. While I'd thrashed around trying to free my bound wrists, I'd smashed Sebastian with my tail. That might have cost him precious seconds—seconds where he could have resurfaced and gulped oxygen.

Not only had he faced his biggest fear to free me, but he might have sacrificed his life to do so. Panic clutched my throat.

No, that wouldn't help. I had to push on.

I flapped my tail hard, propelling me higher. Once I closed in on the shore and broke the surface, I shifted back to human form.

My breathing and body adjusted to the new environment. As I dragged Sebastian onto the sand, flashlights scanned around the house and water, just missing us.

After I lay him on his back, I checked for signs that he'd be okay. But he wasn't breathing!

My muscles froze. The urge to scream rose, but I stifled it. It was more important to try to save him. Forcing myself not to panic, I adjusted his position and applied compressions to his chest and counted along to "Staying Alive" the way I'd learned in a CPR course long ago.

I checked again to see if he started to breathe. No. Nothing.

After two more rescue breaths, I pleaded, "Sebastian, wake up," and resumed compressions. "Don't leave me!"

What else could I do?

I returned to the compressions. Shit, maybe I was doing it wrong. It was one thing to practice in a controlled situation and another when faced with the terror of a life-and-death situation. I scrambled through my brain for the steps. Wait, didn't I hear something about rescue breaths no longer recommended? Then what? I didn't know. My training was outdated. Would I be doing more harm than good?

Bending closer to his ear, I crooned, "Sebastian, come back. Be with me. Be my mate." I put all my intention behind my song, willing him to wake.

I didn't know if it would work. When I'd tried to use my song inside to confuse Jakob, he'd laughed and said my magic wouldn't work on him. Still, I had to try. I'd do anything to save Sebastian.

I continued with the rescue breaths because I didn't know any other options. An unexpected shock stunned me, and I pulled back. Tingles vibrated from my lips down my throat and into my chest. Warmth spread to my limbs, radiating outward to my naked skin.

What the hell was going on?

Stunned, I stared at my hands as I resumed compressions. Magic coursed through me—a kind I'd never felt before.

Sebastian sputtered and coughed up water.

"Sebastian!" I covered my chest.

He coughed some more. I helped turn him to the side, and he pushed out more water. He gasped for breath and then lay on his back in the sand.

"Gianna." His voice sounded hoarse.

"Are you okay?" I fretted over him, touching his cheek and then his chest. His heart beat beneath my fingers.

He forced a weak smile. "I am now." After two more heaving breaths, he added, "Now that you're safe."

"Me?" My heart raced. "Sebastian, you almost drowned to save me!"

"You're worth it." Another deep breath. "You're my ma—" He stopped. "Sorry."

"Don't be." The magic continued to travel through me. I raised my hand. "Do you feel it? The magic?"

A wondrous expression passed over his face. "Do you mean between us?"

That was what it was. This strange sense that we were connected. "Yes."

His mouth curled up into a lopsided smile. "I do."

Choked up with emotion, I brought my fingertips together. "Oh, Sebastian." I lowered my hands. "I feel it. What you tried to tell me." I placed my hand before my heart. "It makes me feel —whole."

His eyes brightened. "I know what you mean. I didn't recognize it as quickly as my wolf, but yes."

I chuckled. "Your wolf is smarter than us both."

Sebastian laughed. "That's what he's been trying to beat into me."

Lights flashed over us. "Who's there?"

I recognized Nova's voice. "It's me, Gianna."

"Gianna!" She rushed over. When she stopped a few feet away, she said, "You're naked. And you're both wet. What's going on? Are you okay?"

I glanced at Sebastian and repeated his line. "I am now."

Nova bent down onto her knees. "I'm so sorry—when Sebastian said you didn't show up, I was super worried. I kept thinking it was like last time, when you were taken by Andre, and I had to do something. I told Zoe about what was going on, and she made some connections. She thought your mother might be involved in some attempts to infiltrate the Network. She said you might be in danger. Zoe and some other witches are searching the area."

Sebastian groaned. He propped himself up to his elbows as if ready to act.

I touched his arm to note everything was all right.

"Zoe was right," I told Nova. "I understand why you told her." I exhaled. "You were right about my mother."

Nova sighed. "I wish I wasn't."

"I know. Me too." I shook my head. "She was just using me."

"Oh, I'm so sorry." She sighed. "What happened?"

I wrapped my arms around myself. "Can you get me a blanket from the house? Then I'll tell you everything."

"Of course." Nova rose and dashed toward the beach house.

I turned to Sebastian. He stared at me with concerned eyes, now crinkling at the edges.

Placing one hand on his face, I caressed it. "You're a crazy wolf. But my kind of crazy."

His eyes brightened. "Without a doubt."

I searched his eyes. "Forget everything I'd said before. I freaked out, and I'm sorry. I want to be with you."

So many emotions passed over his face, I couldn't track them. "I must have drowned and am imagining this."

"No, you were unconscious, but I'm the one truly waking up. I'm letting go of my hang-ups that have kept me from seeing what I want. What I need." I leaned closer to his lips. "You." I kissed him.

The smile he gave me was the brightest I'd ever seen. "Now I definitely know I'm dreaming," he teased.

I laughed. "After I put some clothes on and we tell these witches what happened here tonight, let's go home and curl up in bed for a week."

"Home," he repeated. His warm eyes caressed my face, searching deep inside me. "I'd like that." He furrowed his brows. "Does that mean my place or yours?"

It was kind of odd that I'd phrased it that way. Maybe it was a sign of something that could be in the distant future. "Come to my place and let me take care of you for a change."

SEBASTIAN

I spent two magical days and nights at Gianna's place, most of the time in her bed.

After another hot night with my siren, I rolled onto my side, panting hard. "If this is the reward after nearly drowning, I'll dive headlong into the ocean every day."

She laughed. "You can skip the near-death experience now that I've finally woken up."

I stroked down the side of her smooth side and down over her hips. It still astonished me to see her appearing like a mermaid under the sea. Then again, she'd seen me as a wolf for the first time, which had to be surprising.

"It took me a while to catch on to what my wolf had been telling me all along." I shrugged. "And I struggled with it as well at first."

She gazed into my eyes. "Maybe we both needed something drastic to happen to recognize what was right in front of us, but now we know." She propped herself onto her forearm. "Is your wolf happy now?"

When I hesitated, she prodded, "Sebastian…"

"Yes," I replied. "For the most part."

"Meaning?" Gianna knotted her brows together.

"He's ecstatic that we're together, but—" I paused, knowing this might scare her off, but decided truth was the best option. "But he's pushing for me to mark you."

"Oh." She bit her lip. "The mating bite, right?"

"Yes."

She took in a sharp inhale. "That scares me. It's so—permanent."

"I understand," I assured her, brushing her upper arm. "And I'll never pressure you to do that." I kissed her smooth shoulder. "I'm just happy to be here with you."

OVER THE NEXT FEW WEEKS, we avoided that topic. Although my wolf harped at me about the bite, I told him to be content with what we had. So what if Gianna didn't want me to mark her? At least, we were together.

Still, that instinct was impossible to ignore, especially during sex. My canines emerged as I longed to sink my teeth into the soft flesh near her shoulder.

One evening, I cooked chicken cacciatore for us at my place. The guys were working, and we had the house to ourselves. After we ate, we sat in the living room with a glass of chardonnay watching the fire blaze in the fireplace.

"How about a board game?" Gianna suggested.

"Hmm." I gave her a skeptical glance. "I thought you called them bored-to-death games."

She laughed in agreement. "Yes, but I had fun playing trivia with you guys. Nova told me about your version of Scrabble. Color me intrigued."

"Okay. How about you set up the game while I make us some Mexican hot chocolate?"

"Deal."

While she went down to the basement, I prepared the drinks, filling the top of the mugs with whipped cream. I carried them over to the coffee table where she'd set up the game.

"Smells delicious." She took a sip. "Ooh, it is."

"Glad you like it."

She took the bag of letters and filtered through it, searching for tiles.

"You can't pick your letters," I scoffed.

"I want to spell something." She put down letter tiles starting from the star in the center, spelling out M-A-T-E.

She glanced at me with a serious expression. "Tell me what this means to you, Sebastian."

"Everything," I admitted. "Your mate is your partner. Your other half. There's only one."

She stared at me and nodded. "And you think I'm your mate?"

"I know it." I touched my heart. "With a certainty."

"I feel a connection, too." She swallowed. "Sometimes it scares me." She sipped her hot cocoa and held onto the mug with both hands.

"What about that scares you?"

She sighed. "The label, for one."

"We don't need to use it," I assured her.

She picked up the M. "Maybe we can make it an acronym. Something that isn't so forever sounding."

"Okay," I replied, amused. "Like what?" I took a sip of my drink. The cool whipped cream countered the hot spicy chocolate. A perfect combo.

"Most Awesome, Terrific, Exquisite."

I laughed. "That makes as much sense as some of the lyrics I've heard you sing." Gianna often sang in the shower. Typically, it was nonsense, but it was one of the most endearing things I loved about her—especially as she sang them in her beautiful voice.

"Okay, you come up with something, Shakespeare." She handed me the bag of letters.

"Hmm, let's see." I sifted through the letters and spelled out words down from each letter.

"Make Amazing Torrid Ecstasy?" she read. "You think that's an improvement?"

"Well, it makes more sense."

"How so?"

"The sex is incredible."

She nodded. "I agree."

"Magical," I added. "When you bond with your mate, it's supposed to be this mystical experience."

"Are you talking about the mating bite?"

"Yes. I heard it's the most amazing sex of your life."

"Ooh, magical sex?" She stroked my thigh and chuckled. "Why didn't you tell me that from the beginning? That sounds more pleasurable than the painful bite I've been envisioning."

I worked with the letters to spell out Magical Amazing Torrid Encounter. "Better?"

"Indeed. We're getting there."

I searched her eyes. "Does that mean—you want to?"

Gianna exhaled. "I'm getting more comfortable with the idea." She grinned. "The promise of magical sex is quite enticing." She cocked her head. "Are you okay with waiting?"

"For the woman I love? Of course," I replied.

Her eyes widened with wonder. "You love me?"

"I do," I declared. "With all my heart and soul. I love you, Gianna." I took her hand and kissed it.

She beamed. "I love you, too." She sighed. "I don't want to blow this. What we have is indeed magical."

"No pressure, no rush." Raising my chin, I added, "Besides, the greater the buildup, the greater the reward."

Her lips curled into a sensual smile. "I like how you think, my sexy wolf." She stroked down my cheek. "My mate."

I gaped at her in utmost surprise.

"I wanted to hear how it sounds." She tipped her head. "Mate," she repeated. "I like it. But I also like lover."

"Me, too." I chuckled.

Gianna stood and took my hand. "I think we should start working on the buildup." Her eyes gleamed with dark sensuality as she led me to the stairs up to my room. "And then we'll get ever closer to that reward."

She stirred my desire like no one else could. I followed her up the stairs. I'd follow her anywhere. Once we reached my doorway, I cupped her face with both hands. "I love you, my siren. My lover. My mate." Then I kissed her.

GIANNA

Sebastian slung his arm around my waist as we entered the Danger Zone. Nova, Diego, and Lucas were behind us.

Sebastian said, "I have fond memories here. It's where I met my mate and she tossed me on my ass."

"Well, you were quite the animal that night." I leaned in and whispered. "And even more so every time since."

Billy Idol's "Hot in the City" played, and I remembered singing it in the basement with Nova.

Sebastian murmured in my ear, "It certainly is hot in witch city every night with my siren."

After we headed to the bar, I faced him. "I was thinking about what you said about family."

"What did I say?" he asked.

"That it doesn't have to be who you're born with. You can find your tribe."

He grinned. "Ah, right."

"I think you're right about that." I nodded behind us. "Nova has been like family since we were kids."

"And now you have me."

"I'm glad I found you."

"Me too." He kissed me. "We're all one big hodgepodge in a crazy family."

I laughed. That's how the world might see us—a half-siren, wolf shifter, witch, vampire, and half-dragon shifter. Not the typical crew.

Things were better with my biological family, too, specifically my father. I told him about what happened with my mother, apologizing for not listening to him as he was right to warn me. He apologized as well for deceiving me and being so overbearing in trying to protect me. It was shocking to hear my stern dad saying sorry, but it felt good. Even if it hadn't happened, I'd be okay. I had this crew with me, many who'd risked their lives to save me. I couldn't find a better tribe.

The next song played, Monty Python's "Always Look on the Bright Side of Life," which I'd added to the rotation after we'd watched that ridiculous movie together. The guys sang along, and Nova and I joined in.

"Poor Lucas." I glanced at us lining up at the bar. "Do you think he feels like a fifth wheel?"

Sebastian chuckled. "He's probably laughing at us right now for being fools in love when we could be fielding a partner for the night."

Lucas's gaze roamed the club, appearing as if he was on the prowl to hunt.

"Think he'll ever settle down?"

"I wouldn't call it 'settling.'" Sebastian pulled me close and stared into my eyes. "We need to find a better word for that."

I chuckled. "Guess we have to play Scrabble again."

"Maybe tomorrow." A hungry glimmer gleamed in his eyes. "We can find something more physical to play tonight."

"Indeed." I smiled. "I'm counting on it." I leaned closer and kissed him.

When I pulled back, I searched his warm eyes. "Never would I have thought I'd be here tonight with the wolf shifter who caused a scene in my club the first night we'd met. Now I can't imagine my life without you in it."

Sebastian's sensual mouth widened into a smile. "I'll create a scene whenever and wherever you like."

"Ooh, yes," I murmured. "Tonight. My bedroom."

LUCAS

Surrounded by couples. Yech. I couldn't believe I lost my wingman. Diego had never been down to meet women, but Sebastian and I were a team. Now that he'd found his mate, that meant those days were sadly over.

"You're next, Lucas," Sebastian said. "It's time for you to find your mate."

"Plee-ase," I dismissed. "Unless you mean my companion for the night—which just so happens to be my plan for the evening."

"You know what I mean," Sebastian said.

"No can do." I shook my head. "Just because you abandoned me as my wingman, doesn't mean this dragon is about to stop flying."

"You were my wingman," Sebastian countered.

"Does it matter?" Gianna interrupted.

I circled my hand. "Love you guys, but it's too much couple pheromones over here. I need to go and find my mate," I teased them. While their expressions all brightened with keen interest, I clarified—" My *playmate* for the night."

Then I walked into the crowd, ready to see who wanted to fly high with this dragon tonight.

A NOTE FROM THE AUTHOR:

Find out what fate has in store for Lucas in Dancing with My Elf, *book 3 in the Salem Supernaturals series!*

Sign up for my newsletter at lisacarlislebooks.com for the latest releases and receive a welcome gift with free books!

GO BEHIND THE SCENES

Want more from the stories? Want to be the first to read new books before they're released?

Join me at Patreon to go behind the scenes with music, videos, signed books, and exclusive content!

https://www.patreon.com/lisacarlisle

CONNECTED SERIES

Want more wolf shifters, witches, vampires, and demons? This Salem Supernaturals series is connected to the White Mountain Shifters trilogy. Find out more about Sebastian's former pack as three wolf shifters from a rival pack find their fated mates—and a whole lot of trouble. And read more about witches from the Salem Supernatural Network as they try to ease tensions between packs and meet someone unexpected... Book one is The Reluctant Wolf and His Fated Mate.

Salem Supernaturals is also connected to the Underground Encounters series, featuring supernaturals at an underground club north of Boston. You'll return to Salem for more paranormal romance featuring cursed witches and shifters, vampires, demons, and rockstars!

BOOK LIST

Salem Supernaturals

A witch without magic inherits a house with quirky roommates, and magical sparks fly!

- *Rebel Spell*
- *Hot in Witch City*
- *Dancing with My Elf*
- *Night Wedding*
- *Bite Wedding*

White Mountain Shifters

Howls Romance

Fated mates and forbidden love. When wolf shifters find their fated mate, the trouble is only just beginning.

- *The Reluctant Wolf and His Fated Mate*
- *The Wolf and His Forbidden Witch*
- *The Alpha and His Enemy Wolf*
- All three available in the White Mountain Shifters set

Underground Encounters

Steamy paranormal romances set in an underground goth club that attracts vampires, witches, shifters, and gargoyles.

- *Book 1: SMOLDER (a vampire / firefighter romance)*
- *Book 2: FIRE (a witch / firefighter romance)*
- *Book 3: IGNITE (a feline shifter / rock star romance)*
- *Book 4: BURN (a vampire / shapeshifter rock romance)*

- *Book 5: HEAT (a gargoyle shifter romance)*
- *Book 6: BLAZE (a gargoyle shifter rockstar romance)*
- *Book 7: COMBUST (vampire / witch romances)*
- *Book 8: INFLAME (a gargoyle shifter / witch romance)*
- *Book 9: TORCH (a gargoyle shifter / werewolf romance*
- *Book 10: SCORCH (an incubus vs succubus demon romance)*

Chateau Seductions

An art colony on a remote New England island lures creative types—
and supernatural characters. Steamy paranormal romances.

- *Darkness Rising*
- *Dark Velvet*
- *Dark Muse*
- *Dark Stranger*
- *Dark Pursuit*

Highland Gargoyles

Gargoyle shifters, wolf shifters, and tree witches have divided the Isle
of Stone after a great battle 25 years ago. One risk changes it all…

- *Knights of Stone: Mason*
- *Knights of Stone: Lachlan*
- *Knights of Stone: Bryce*
- *Seth: a wolf shifter romance in the series*
- *Knights of Stone: Calum*
- *Knights of Stone: Gavin*

Stone Sentries

Meet your perfect match the night of the super moon — or your
perfect match for the night. A cop teams up with a gargoyle shifter
when demons attack Boston.

- *Tempted by the Gargoyle*
- *Enticed by the Gargoyle*
- *Captivated by the Gargoyle*

Anchor Me

Second chance military romances! Three military brothers meet their matches while in Newport, RI.

- *Angelo*
- *Vince*
- *Matty*
- *Jack*
- *Slade*
- *Mark*

Night Eagle Operations

A paranormal romantic suspense novel

- *When Darkness Whispers*

Berkano Vampires

A shared author world with dystopian paranormal romances.

- *Immortal Resistance*

Blood Courtesans

A shared author world with the vampire blood courtesans.

- *Pursued: Mia*

Visit LisaCarlisleBooks.com to learn more!

ACKNOWLEDGMENTS

As always, I am tremendously grateful to everyone who helps make each book possible, helping me shape the strange ideas in my head into a coherent story. Huge thanks to my critique partners, editors, beta readers, proofreaders, ARC readers, Street Team, and you, the reader! Thank you for spending time with me in these worlds with characters I love.

ABOUT THE AUTHOR

USA Today bestselling author Lisa Carlisle loves stories with dark, brooding heroes and independent heroines. Her romances have been named Top Picks at Night Owl Reviews and the Romance Reviews.

When she was younger, she worked in a variety of jobs, moving to various countries. She backpacked alone through Europe, and lived in Paris before returning to the U.S. She owned a bookstore for a few years as she loves to read. She's now married to a fantastic man, and they have two kids, two cats, and too many fish.

Visit her website for more on books, trailers, playlists, and more:

Lisacarlislebooks.com

Sign up for her newsletter to hear about new releases, specials, and freebies:

http://www.lisacarlislebooks.com/subscribe/

Lisa loves to connect with readers. You can find her on:

Facebook

Twitter

Pinterest

Instagram

Goodreads